'Consider the garden still yours.'

'I'd like that, Mr Howard.'

'My friends call me Jonathan,' he said. 'Do you think you could try? Or do you prefer B.J.?'

'Just while you're here,' Troy said, knowing she was floundering. His presence blotted out everything. It was all she could do not to touch his hands, tell him that they would be all right soon, that they would heal naturally, and that he would be a great surgeon again.

Dear Reader

We don't travel far this month, but there is compensation in welcoming back Elizabeth Harrison after a long absence—also Stella Whitelaw and Janet Ferguson. The warmth they generate between their characters is lovely, and I'm sure you'll find their romances fascinating. We also have Caroline Anderson back again after the mammoth work she put into her trilogy, moving out of the hospital setting to explore the problems encountered by a working mother in general practice. Lots of pleasurable reading!

The Editor

Stella Whitelaw's writing career began when she was a cub reporter on a local newspaper. She became one of the first and youngest women chief reporters in London. While bringing up her small children, she had many short stories published in magazines. She is deeply interested in alternative medicines, and is pleased that her son, now a doctor and anaesthetist, has an open mind about them. A painful slipped disc has improved since practising the Alexander Technique daily.

Recent titles by the same author:

DRAGON LADY
THIS SAVAGE SKY

A CERTAIN HUNGER

BY
STELLA WHITELAW

MILLS & BOON LIMITED
ETON HOUSE   18–24 PARADISE ROAD
RICHMOND   SURREY   TW9 1SR

To Cait
a good friend

All the characters in this book have no existence outside the imagination of the Author, and have no relation whatsoever to anyone bearing the same name or names. They are not even distantly inspired by any individual known or unknown to the Author, and all the incidents are pure invention.

All Rights Reserved. The text of this publication or any part thereof may not be reproduced or transmitted in any form or by any means, electronic or mechanical, including photocopying, recording, storage in an information retrieval system, or otherwise, without the written permission of the publisher.

This book is sold subject to the condition that it shall not, by way of trade or otherwise, be lent, resold, hired out or otherwise circulated without the prior consent of the publisher in any form of binding or cover other than that in which it is published and without a similar condition including this condition being imposed on the subsequent purchaser.

*First published in Great Britain 1993
by Mills & Boon Limited*

© Stella Whitelaw 1993

*Australian copyright 1993
Philippine copyright 1993
This edition 1993*

ISBN 0 263 78186 0

*Set in 10 on 12 pt Linotron Times
03-9307-50291*

*Typeset in Great Britain by Centracet, Cambridge
Made and printed in Great Britain*

CHAPTER ONE

SHE tugged at the sashes of the old-fashioned window and flung it open, letting the sea wind rush in and feather her overheated brow. Troy was angry, almost beyond coherent words. Grace was making her give up her home and it was not fair.

Troy leaned further out over the wide sill till she could touch the tree whose long, tapering branches often tapped mysterious messages on her window-pane. The new leaves were curled tightly like pale green gloves. When Troy had first moved into Coastguard Cottage, she had been afraid of the insistent tapping, as if it were a menace, but gradually she had come to realise that the tree's messages were friendly.

'I'm being sent away,' she complained now to the tree. Her indignation boiled over again. 'Like one of the girls. . .expelled for bad behaviour to some dingy attic flat over the science wing. I don't deserve it. All those revolting smells floating up from the labs. I shall hate it, especially after living in this cottage, having it all to myself, and with the sea so near.'

Grace Howard had been a good friend and so supportive when Troy Kingsbury had joined the staff of Belling Hills, an expensive girls' boarding-school on the Devon coast, the year before. It had been a relief to all when Troy had taken on the responsibility of the health care of four hundred girls and the many problems that arose from being the daughters of wealthy and often much married parents. Along with the post had come the offer of a small cottage on the estate, and Troy had been elated at the prospect of her own home at last.

'But now I'm having to move out, lock, stock and several bottles of good French wine, at two days' notice. Can you believe it? And all because of a man.'

The thought of leaving the cottage was like a knife in the ribs. Although she did not own it, she had come to think of it as permanent, as her real home. These few rooms, the pounding sea outside and the tiny cliff-edge garden were the essence of her present calm. They had eased, shaped and brought her to a state of contentment that had been missing in the turmoil of the years before.

She had watched the whitebeam's vibrancy through all the seasons, seen the sea's fiercely changing moods, rejoiced in its turbulence and its calm. She had changed too. The cottage had been the cocoon in which she'd evolved from a nervous wreck into a slim, maturer woman who coped with emergencies with confidence, her head held high, a ready smile on her sweetly curved mouth.

But now she had to go. It was only for three months, but it was long enough to seem endless. She leaned against the window-frame and stared at her tree, hoping that time had somehow stopped and the unwelcome news had all been part of a disastrous dream.

Bad dreams had once been an every night occurrence. Troy had lost her husband to an ambitious and elegant career woman, and then her home through the trauma of repossession. Foolish and handsome Peter — she could almost feel sorry for him and the desperate situation he had got himself into. But it had not been funny at the time. Her husband had been unable to extract himself from his financial tangle, let alone the emotional one, and had conveniently forgotten to keep up the mortgage repayments on their Edwardian semi-detached house. It had all come as a terrible shock, losing husband, then home. There was no way Troy could have taken on the burden of the repayments on her salary as a ward sister at a sprawling concrete rabbit-warren hospital in North London.

She had not even been able to talk to Peter about it, remind him of his responsibilities. By that time he had been on his way to Corfu with the expensive Fiona and had been too besotted to care much if Troy was homeless.

Troy could hardly bring herself to remember those days. She had been overworking to the point of exhaustion, then a bad dose of influenza had brought her mentally and physically low. She had stared down a black tunnel in her mind and had longed to escape through it to somewhere else.

'But they found me in time,' she told the tree. 'Wasn't that lucky? Thank goodness for the smoke alarm in the kitchen.'

It had sent its shrill call into the evening air as her supper had burnt to cinders under the grill. She did not know even now whether she had meant to take all those paracetamols or whether in the daze of tiredness and flu symptoms she had simply forgotten and taken the pills twice or even three times, both on the ward and at home. She simply could not remember.

She remembered going home on the bus when her shift had ended, buying some chops at a late-night supermarket and letting herself into the empty house. She had known she was ill, and had planned to eat and then go straight to bed.

Her neighbours, hearing the alarm and seeing smoke through the kitchen window, had gone in immediately. Troy had not even locked the door. They had found her sprawled on the bedroom floor.

It was while convalescing from the flu that Troy had seen the adverstisement for a fully qualified nursing sister at an exclusive girls' boarding-school on the coast. The last phrase of the advertisement had stood out in neon lights. 'Accommodation available'. A small coastguard's cottage on the edge of the sea went with the job.

Troy had loved the cottage on sight — the weather-beaten stone, the salt-blistered paint, the windows glistening with spray at high tide when the big waves pounded the cliff below. And the tiny garden, full of sea-clover and cowslips, only big enough for a deck-chair and the graceful whitebeam, the tree that became her confidant. That one day the cliff would erode and the garden slide into the sea was immaterial.

Grace Howard, the headmistress of Belling Hills, had been delighted to offer Troy the job.

'You are just the kind of person we need here,' she said at the interview. 'The girls will take to you, I know that. You're young enough to relate to them. And it's so important for the parents to know that we have a really well qualified sister in charge. It puts their minds at rest. So many of them live abroad and we have to be prepared to cope with any emergency, from cuts and bruises to epidemics.'

'And the cottage goes with the job?' Troy asked. The repossession date had passed—a day of relentless agony. She had put her furniture in store and taken a bed-sitter in the nurses' annexe.

'Yes, it belongs to the school. This was once quite a big estate, though bits and pieces have been sold off at times. We've always hung on to the old cottage, probably because it has little commercial value. It's very quaint, though, with lots of character.'

'You mean an outdoor loo?'

'Oh, no,' Grace laughed. 'The second bedroom upstairs has been modernised as a bathroom. It's very comfortable really. Just right for a single person.'

Troy winced at the word, but, as soon as the divorce went through, that was what she would be. She had already reverted to her maiden name. She never wanted to think of Peter again.

'Could you start next term?'

'Yes,' said Troy.

Now all that quiet calm had erupted with Grace's sudden announcement when Troy was summoned to her office. She wanted Troy to move out of the cottage for three months so that her brother could live there.

'I know you won't mind,' said Grace, quite oblivious to the indignant gleam in Troy's green eyes. 'It's not for long. But my brother has been in this horrendous helicopter accident, and unless we can get him away from the pressure of his work he's going to take twice as long to recover. He needs peace and quiet and motivation to persevere with his physiotherapy. Apparently he's just not turning up for his appointments in London. Says he's too busy.'

'How very foolish,' said Troy, deliberately using the same word that she associated with her husband. 'Where shall I move to? Perhaps there's an inn in the village?'

'Oh, heavens, no, you needn't go to any expense on our behalf,' enthused Grace, still oblivious to Troy's true feelings. 'You can have the attic over the science lab. It's perfectly habitable. I'll get Joe to clear out the rubbish and give it a lick of paint.'

'Wonderful,' said Troy, drily.

'Thank you, my dear. I knew I could rely on your good nature. You're always so helpful.'

Troy wandered round the cottage now, lost and aimless. She did not know where to start with her packing. She had taken some of her own furniture out of store and gathered a few new domestic items and ornaments, as well as all her clothes and piles of books. It certainly would not all fit into that poky flat over the science lab. The year at Belling Hills had given her a chance to rebuild a home around her. Now she had to dismantle it for the sake of some wayward invalid who would not keep his physio appointments.

The loft was the answer. Although the cottage was small with only two rooms upstairs and two down, there was ample crawling-about space under the roof, and access to it was through a trapdoor in the bathroom ceiling. She would be able to reach it easily if she stood on the bathroom stool. For once her height was an asset.

She tried to calm her anger as she emptied drawers and folded clothes into suitcases and carrier bags. She hoped there weren't bats or mice in the loft. She would sue Mr Howard if anything got eaten or went mouldy.

The bathroom stool was just high enough for Troy to reach the trapdoor, push it open, and somehow lever her belongings into the loft. It was hard work and soon she was perspiring with the effort. She was so busy that she did not hear a car draw up, voices, then the door of the cottage opening.

Nor did she hear someone call, 'Hello. Anyone there?'

Troy was balanced precariously on the stool, a heavy suitcase halfway in, when the door to the bathroom was flung open. It knocked the stool and she went flying. So did the suitcase.

She was caught by a pair of strong arms that broke her fall and stopped her from joining the suitcase on the floor. Troy found herself pulled hard against a warm, broad male chest in a grip that was both firm and decisive, yet more dependent on the strength of muscled arms than on the hands.

She struggled vigorously. 'Let go of me,' Troy gasped. 'Who are you, anyway? Who are you? Get out. This is private property. If you don't go, I'll call the police.'

'That's a little premature and not necessary. I did call out.'

'You'd better explain — what are you doing here?' she demanded.

'And are you going to tell me what you're doing in my loft?' asked the stranger laconically.

'Your loft?'

Troy's eyes widened. She pushed the man away and stood back in the confined space. The conversion had not left much space for a confrontation between two irate adults. There was hardly passing room. The man did not look like an intruder. He was tall and well dressed in a light grey suit, with opaque sunglasses hiding his eyes, his glossy dark hair groomed and neatly barbered. He stood in the doorway with a sort of lazy insolence.

'Mr Howard?' she asked tentatively.

'Yes, Jonathan Howard.'

She took a deep breath, pulling herself together. So this was Grace's brother. She knew she looked a mess in ancient denims and washed-out shirt, her long brown hair escaping from a butterfly clip, her face probably streaked with dust and cobwebs. 'You're two days too early,' she retorted. 'I'm not ready to move out.'

'I had the opportunity of a lift down,' he said. 'Since I'm not driving at the moment, it seemed too good a chance to miss. Perhaps I can help you pack?'

He indicated the fallen suitcase which had burst open. All sorts of intimate and frothy garments were spilling out — relics of long-lost honeymoon days. It also contained sensible winter thermals which she hurriedly pushed back into the case, out of sight.

'I don't need your help,' said Troy in her most authoritative manner. 'The way out is down the stairs and through the front door.'

He looked vaguely amused and leaned against the door post. 'Grace said you might be prickly.'

Troy picked up a carrier-bag of winter sweaters and threw them into the loft as if they were part of Mr Howard's anatomy. The family resemblance was strong. He and Grace were both tall, angular people; Grace had the same aquiline nose and heavy eyebrows.

He took off his sunglasses and Troy found herself looking into eyes of the deepest blue. They were a vivid colour, bluer than the sea outside, and such a contrast to his tanned skin. He'd been abroad somewhere to pick up that tan, Troy thought enviously, knowing she couldn't afford a holiday anywhere, not even a day on Brighton pier.

'You don't look ill,' she said.

'Have you X-ray eyes or shall I undress, Sister?'

'That won't be at all necessary,' she said, not bothering to conceal the dislike in her voice. He was far too good-looking, too assured, too mocking. 'Grace told me you'd been in a helicopter accident. I expected a wheelchair case at the least. When are you planning to move in?'

'As soon as possible, if that's convenient for you. My cases are downstairs with my computer. I could help you carry your things over to the main school. I understand it's no distance,' he added pointedly.

'The attic flat isn't ready yet. It's got to be cleared out,' said Troy stubbornly.

'So Grace told me, but she has a spare room in her apartment where you could sleep until then.'

Troy could not believe the insolence of the man.

'Why don't you have the spare room?' she said, gritting her teeth.

'In a girls' school?' he said, raising his eyebrows fractionally. 'All those young ladies running around in short tennis skirts. It would put up my blood-pressure.'

'Nonsense,' said Troy briskly. 'It would only be for a few days.'

He nodded in agreement. 'As you say, it would only be for a few days, and then you will be safely ensconced in your little eyrie.'

'I am not a bat or a witch, nor a bird of prey, Mr Howard,' said Troy, wondering how long she could hold on to her temper. 'And I should prefer to remain in this cottage. Are you sure you couldn't make other arrangements? After all, you seem respectable enough to stay at a hotel. I'm sure you'd have no trouble finding one that would take you in.'

'But Grace would object strongly,' he said. 'She wants to keep an eye on me, to make sure I keep taking the medicine, do my exercises. You know what sisters are.'

'No, I don't. But I do know what babies some men can be. My years in Men's Surgical taught me that. Some faint clean clean away at the sight of an injection needle.'

'Not uncommon. I may have done it myself. I'm sorry I can't drive you up to the school. Someone will be bringing my car down in a few days.'

'Lost your licence?' Troy asked flippantly, recalling the computer and a pressurised job in London. . . He sounded like a yuppie stockbroker. 'Too many champagne lunches? Speeding on a motorway?'

'No, severed tendons of both hands. The nerves will take several months to heal, as you know. They regrow at the rate of about one millimetre a day. It'll be some time before the feeling returns.'

Troy did not know where to look. She felt about two inches high, faint with shame, and a wave of nausea hit her at the thought of his injury. He retrieved her from embarrassment with a self-mocking remark.

'I'll live to lift another glass of Campari,' he said.

'I'm so sorry,' she said awkwardly. 'Grace didn't tell me much except that you'd been in an accident. Of course you need time. The keyboard will help. . .or a typewriter or piano. . .anything to exercise your fingers.'

'The word processor is to work on. I don't intend to completely waste my time down here. I've work to do. That's another reason why I couldn't live in the school or a hotel. The noise would be unbearable.'

Troy could see that it was all sewn up. She might as well get on with the next three months and hope she was too busy to miss her cottage. All those long summer evenings. . . She couldn't see herself enjoying the sea air with a good book and a glass of chilled wine at her side in an attic flat.

'I suppose I might as well get the move over since you've offered to help,' she said. 'I don't have a car. You can use my new microwave while you're here. Do you know how to use one?'

'I can read instructions.'

'There's a booklet alongside it which gives you times and power rate. They save on the washing-up.'

'Thank you. I promise to be careful with it. Can you drive?'

Troy thought of Peter's company BMW. She had learned to drive in it, but of course he had taken the car with him when he'd moved in with Fiona. 'Yes, I can drive. Why?'

'Grace is hoping you'll drive me to physiotherapy for treatment twice a week. There's a very good physiotherapy department at the hospital in Totnes. But I need to get there.'

Troy was taken aback by the casual way her life was being rearranged. Grace had not mentioned any chauffeuring. 'I can't promise,' she said, carrying a case downstairs. 'I can't promise. It's not easy to leave the school if I'm needed here and I'm on duty with a bleeper twenty-four hours.'

'Naturally. We'll see how it works out. I don't want to be a nuisance to you. I'm not keen on going anyway.'

A reluctant patient. Troy could understand why Grace was worried. Lots of men reacted like that, refusing treatment or being antagonistic to good advice. Well, she wasn't going to be his minder. He was a grown man and could look after himself.

The bleeper went off in her pocket. 'Excuse me, I'm wanted. I'll give you the cottage keys later.'

'I may as well come with you and carry something.'

She piled some books into his arms. She did not know if he could grip the handle of a case. 'This way.'

It was not a long walk along the lane and across the newly mown playing-fields to the school. Troy knew she could do it in seven minutes. The medical centre was on the ground floor of what had once been the stables of a big house, looking out on to a paved courtyard. Grace had her apartment in the main house, where the staff's rooms and library were situated, with most of the ground floor being used as offices and reception area and sixth-form classrooms.

Troy was proud of her surgery. It had been a small, dismal room when she had arrived, but now, with Joe's help, it was a bright, cheerful room with posters on the walls, books to read and several comfortable chairs, as well as a treatment couch, medical cabinet and her desk. She liked to make the girls feel at home and there was always tea and biscuits for a tearful patient.

A small huddle of girls stood in the courtyard outside the medical centre. Troy got out her keys, spotting her patient immediately.

She knew Melanie Brown well. She was an energetic twelve-year-old, already vice-captain of the middle school netball team. She spent every waking hour practising on the courts, shooting and dodging an opponent. But this afternoon she had come to grief. Blood was pouring from her mouth and down her white shirt, and she was crying. Her friends clustered around her, getting in the way.

'What's happened to Melanie?' asked Troy briskly. 'Can someone tell me? Not all at once. Jane?'

'She's lost a front tooth, Sister. She looks awful. She looks horrible. There's just a big gap.'

'Will she have to wear false teeth, Sister?'

Fresh tears from Melanie accompanied this cheering news. She was obviously as keen on preserving her looks as scoring goals. Troy ushered Melanie into the surgery and took her straight over to the basin to wash out the blood.

'Has anyone got the tooth?' she asked.

The girls looked stunned. They turned to each other.

'Miss Richmond, the PE teacher...did she pick it up?'

'She wasn't there. We were just practising when Melanie cannoned into the post. It was an accident, really it was.'

'Of course it was; now I just want that tooth. And fast. Put it in this cup of milk. Don't handle it. Don't wash it. Hold it by the crown and not the root — that's the pointed end. Don't do anything with it but bring it straight back to me.'

'I won't have to wear false teeth, will I?' Melanie wept, sticking her tongue in the gap.

'No, you won't if your friends hurry and find that tooth.'

'I'll go with them,' Jonathan offered.

He strode along with the girls towards the practise courts, and Troy was pleased that he had taken the initiative. At least an adult around would mean a careful search and a fast return of the lost tooth.

'Don't worry, Melanie,' said Troy. 'I'm going to try and put the tooth back in. Then we'll pack you off to the dentist and he can do the rest.'

She phoned through to the staffroom to see who was available with a car. As soon as transport was arranged, she turned to Melanie and cleaned her up, but did nothing to her mouth, letting the girl rinse out the blood over the basin. She had calmed down now, and was a little easier as Troy reassured her.

'They'll call me Gappy,' she insisted.

'No, they won't. You won't have a gap. Cheer up, here comes the search-party. I think they've found it.'

Troy smiled at the triumphant group and then shooed everyone out of the way. They wanted to watch, but Troy knew she needed complete peace and quiet for a delicate operation.

'May I stay?' Jonathan asked.

'Are you sure you won't faint?' said Troy, not really wanting an audience, but he did not look as if he was going to leave.

'Positive,' he said.

The tooth was dirty, so she rinsed it carefully in milk, holding it by the crown. When Melanie was comfortably seated, head back and her mouth open, Troy gently pushed it back into its socket, making sure it was the right way round.

'I've never seen that done before,' said Jonathan, with grudging admiration.

'It's usually painless if it's done immediately after the accident. It's important not to clean the tooth with disinfectant or let the tooth dry out. Now, Melanie, bite on this clean handkerchief and we'll get you to the dentist.'

Troy switched on her computer and brought up Melanie Brown's record on the small screen, and read the details quickly. 'I think I'll give you a tetanus injection, just in case. This won't hurt. Just a tiny pin-prick.'

Melanie nodded, her mouth full of handkerchief. Troy wrote out some notes and gave them to Mrs

Lawson, the history teacher taking Melanie to the dentist.

'Why don't you go with her?' Jonathan asked.

'I'm not really needed and I don't have a car,' said Troy. 'Besides, it's very difficult for me to leave here. I have to be around in case something else happens.'

'You mean you never have any time off?'

'Yes, of course, I have days off, but this isn't one of them. Now, if you'll excuse me, I'd like to clean up. There'll be more girlish hysterics if my next wobbly patient is confronted by a basinful of blood.'

Jonathan Howard watched as she hurried round. It annoyed her immensely that he should just stand and watch. Deliberately she made a lot of noise and clatter, hoping he would get tired of it and go away.

'Why don't I help out?' he said at last. 'I shall have time on my hands.' Quickly, he corrected himself. 'Not exactly on my hands—they're pretty useless—but I still have a brain and legs that work.'

'What on earth are you talking about?' said Troy, wiping round the basin and throwing the disposable cloth away. 'I don't want an assistant, especially some amateur do-gooder. What makes you think you could be of any use to me whatsoever?'

'I could keep the records for you. I know how to work that machine.'

'Big deal, Mr Howard. Wonderful. Why don't you keep out of my way and we'll get along just fine?'

'If that's what you want, Sister. But I would have thought that a willing amateur would be better than nothing. It seems to me that you have a lot of responsibility.'

'The local GPs support me adequately. I can call a doctor to the school in twenty minutes and we have a GP surgery every Friday morning.'

'Excellent. But I still think I could be useful. Sometimes even twenty minutes is a long time.'

Troy turned on him, exasperated. She had had enough of Mr Howard for one day. She was going to be seeing him twice a week too often if she had to take him to Totnes hospital for his treatment.

'Please go away, Mr Howard,' she said. 'I don't need your help. Go and play with your computer, or whatever you do.'

He shrugged his shoulders. 'Just as you please.'

He was turning to go when Grace Howard appeared in the doorway, her face alight with pleasure. She looked as if she had been hurrying, her fine grey hair escaping from its regulation knot.

'Jonathan, dear! I've only just heard that you've arrived. That's marvellous. And you've met our excellent Sister Kingsbury, who keeps everything ticking over and copes with every emergency.'

'Grace, you're looking well.' He gave his sister a warm hug, and an expression of affection crossed his face. 'It's great to see you. And yes, I have met Sister Kingsbury and I'm most impressed. I have even learned what to do with a lost tooth.'

'And what do you think of my baby brother?' asked Grace, taking his arm. Troy winced. She supposed he was about sixteen years younger than Grace. It was difficult to tell. With his height and frame, he was far from being a baby.

'He's definitely grown,' said Troy ironically.

Grace laughed. 'I think he'll just about fit into the cottage. It's so sweet of you to give it up, Troy. I know Jonathan appreciates it. We all want him to get better and return to his work.'

'Of course,' said Troy with a straight face. 'Now if you'll excuse me, I've some medication to give out following this morning's surgery.'

'Jonathan could help you once he's settled in.'

'It's very kind,' said Troy, popping pills into labelled containers as she checked the prescription list on the screen. 'All these offers of help. I'm overwhelmed, but the last person I want around is a well-meaning amateur.'

The smile faded fractionally from Grace's face. She gave a little laugh. 'I wouldn't regard Jonathan as exactly an amateur,' she said. 'He might not have much experience in your kind of nursing, Troy, but he is, after all, Mr Jonathan Howard, one of this country's foremost consultant orthopaedic surgeons. Surely you've heard of him? That's why it's so important that he regain the use of his hands. He can't operate without full feeling in all his fingers.'

Troy's heart sank almost without trace. Her hands stopped in mid-air and she dared not look anywhere except at the tiled floor. Of course she had heard of him, but they had always called him B. J. Howard at her training hospital. Bones and Joints. She had never formally met him, only once catching a glimpse of his tall back in operating greens striding along a corridor. She remembered that day well. There had been something, even then, that had made it difficult for her to take her eyes off him.

CHAPTER TWO

TROY made herself concentrate on her breathing to make sure it went on happening. Her panic subsided. There was no way that she could have known. So Grace's brother was *the* B. J. Howard, and she had waffled on in a stupid, patronising manner about skilled medical assistance when he was one of the most daring orthopaedic surgeons in Europe. Tales of his innovations had percolated down to the nurses who cared for his patients on the wards.

'I should be delighted to avail myself of Mr Howard's assistance or advice if I need it,' said Troy, carefully choosing her words. 'But since he is here for peace and quiet, he'll hardly want to be involved in my day-to-day duties. The school can be very noisy.'

'Exactly,' said Grace, relieved. 'I was sure you could both work something out and you have, and that's wonderful.'

'My car will be down here in a few days,' said Jonathan, his eyes riveted on Troy. 'I've told Sister Kingsbury that she can drive it whenever she wants to.'

'Lucky girl,' said Grace. 'I wish I had the nerve. Come and have some tea, Jonathan, and tell me what you've been doing. We've a lot to catch up on. Perhaps Troy will find time to show you round the school after she has finished her evening surgery.'

Troy produced a frosty smile. It was the last thing she really wanted to do.

'I'm sure. . . Troy. . .has her hands full without being a tour guide to an invalid. I'll find my own way round.' He used her name with a slight query in his voice. People were always curious.

'A nickname from my school-days,' Troy explained. 'My real name is Helen. We were studying the legends and myths of Greece at the time, and my friends got carried away.'

'It suits you,' said Jonathan, acknowledging her long, glossy brown hair and expressive green eyes. 'Your school-friends chose well. It has far more character than B. J. But then I had little say in the matter.'

So he *had* known. Troy could not resist a dimpled smile to herself. 'Count yourself lucky that we didn't call you Bony, the traditional orthopaedic abbreviation. Now if you'll excuse me. . .'

Troy was suddenly aware of her unkempt and casual appearance. A quick glance told her that she had also lost a button off her shirt and that her cleavage was probably the cause of the amusement in his eyes. She stiffened, setting her shoulders into disapproval. The button must have come off when she'd fallen from the bathroom stool. He could have told her. There were such things as safety-pins. 'I need to change into my uniform before the girls start arriving.'

'Thank you for being so co-operative, Troy,' said Grace yet again. 'I'm sure my brother appreciates it.'

Jonathan's mouth curved into a wicked smile. 'And for your future co-operation,' he added.

Some chance, thought Troy. This was getting out of

hand. Any minute now Grace would suggest some other way in which Troy could help the great B. J. rehabilitate.

She hurried into the small shower-room that led from her office, pulling off her shirt and denims. She had two uniforms — a tailored navy dress with crisp white cuffs and silver-buckled belt for formal occasions, and a cornflower-blue trouser-suit with tunic top for surgeries and the sick-bay. She felt she looked less intimidating in the slimly cut trousers, and they were comfortable for getting around the school. She wore nothing on her head, believing frilly caps to be outdated, but she did twist her long hair up into a topknot and secure it with a big butterfly clip. One of the girls had given her a blue flowered clip, and sometimes she wore this to keep her hair back.

She pinned on her RNS brooch, put surgical scissors in the pocket, and looked out along the corridor that served as a waiting-room. Several girls were already waiting. It was not particularly comfortable, but she did provide books, jigsaws and magazines. No one had to wait long.

'Come in, Angela,' she said to the first girl. 'How has your ear been today?'

'I think it still hurts.'

'You only think. . . Don't you know?' said Troy, peering carefully into the girl's ear. The outer canal did not look inflamed. She put in some soothing ear drops. 'I think you've been doing too much jumping into the pool. Sometimes the chlorinated water can irritate the ear.'

'Are you going to stop me swimming?'

'Yes, for a few days. But we'll get Dr Wright to have a look at it tomorrow morning when he's here. I think he ought to take a look. I'll give you a note for both your class teacher and PE.'

She gave Angela a spoonful of paracetamol syrup. 'Ask a member of the care staff for a hot-water bottle wrapped in a towel, and sleep with your ear against it. It'll be comforting and help you to sleep.'

'Thank you, Sister.'

Dr Roger Wright was the youngest of a group of GPs with a group practice on the outskirts of Dartmouth. Troy knew he enjoyed his weekly trips to Belling Hills, not only for the excellent coffee and change of scene away from the bustling clinic, but also for the chance of a few hours of Troy's company. She was well aware that he stretched his visits to the limit, and sometimes she had to practically push him out of the sick-bay. He was a pleasant young man, a conscientious doctor and amiable company, but as far as Troy was concerned the relationship was purely professional.

The last girl waiting in the corridor was Lucy Warren, a new and rather shy pupil. Troy had not spoken to her before, although her records were on file. Troy brought the records on to the screen. Lucy was an only child, with both parents living in London involved in high-powered jobs. Lucy's health was generally good.

She was a freckly girl with a brace on her front teeth and sandy eyelashes. Her hair was a pale reddish blonde, and one day she would be lovely.

'Hello, Lucy. Come in and sit down. How can I help you?'

'I've got a headache, Sister.'
'How long have you had it?'
'All day.'
'Do you feel sick at all? Have you been sick?'
'No.'
'Have you knocked your head at all, fallen down or bumped it?'

Lucy shook her head, but that movement was obviously painful. Troy felt carefully over the girl's head. There were no irregularities. She also made a simple eye test, but could find nothing obviously wrong with Lucy's eyesight.

'Are you eating properly? Not on some silly diet, are you? Are you sleeping well or are you reading under the blankets at night?'

'No.' All Lucy's answers were monosyllabic.

'I don't think there's anything seriously wrong with you. A plain, common or garden nuisance headache.' She gave Lucy two junior soluble aspirins to take straight away and two more to take at bedtime.

'I think you're old enough and sensible enough to take these tablets when you go to bed,' said Troy, putting them into a tiny envelope and writing Lucy's full name on the outside. 'I could come and find you, but you might get teased by the other girls. Headaches seem to be this term's joke. Last term it was piles.'

Lucy seemed pleased with the responsibility and put the packet in her skirt pocket. Then she thanked Troy. She had nice manners.

'Come back if it hasn't cleared by tomorrow. Dr Wright can have a look at you.'

Troy cleared up, finished her notes, and locked the

medicine cabinet. Lucy was probably homesick, as it was her first term away from home and doting parents. They probably spoilt her and neglected her at the same time. She must make a point of talking to the girl. Troy took a fitness club once a week, then there were her health classes. Lucy would be at one of them. They were a popular extra activity, especially the fitness club, where the girls bounced around to the latest pop tunes.

The part-time night nurse, Karen Norwood, would be arriving soon. She was a capable mother of two youngsters, who liked night work. It suited her family commitments. Troy left some messages for her on the desk, asking her to check Angela's ear and that Lucy had taken the aspirin, and explaining what had happened to Melanie Brown. Karen would have an easy night. There was no one in the sick-bay. Troy looked round the small four-bedded ward with satisfaction. It was an attractive room with yellow floral curtains and nice sea pictures on the wall. She liked to see it empty; it meant all the pupils in her care were staying healthy.

Her feet turned automatically towards the cottage before she remembered she didn't live there any more. Grace's spare room was her temporary home before she flew off to the lab attic with her potions and brews.

There were still quite a few personal belongings to collect from the cottage bathroom and kitchen. She might as well do it now. She would leave Mr B. J. Howard some coffee and tea for his breakfast, perhaps some cereal and milk if she was feeling particularly generous. He looked as if he was hopeless at shopping.

He probably had a housekeeper or an adoring female in tow.

Her heart lurched as she realised that any such adoring females would follow him to Devon in droves. What woman could keep away? She resigned herself to a bevy of London beauties weekending in her cottage, in her bedroom, in her bed.

The thought burned like a brand. She was unable to think clearly as images flashed through her mind of hips touching, thighs touching. Could she insist that they did not sleep in her bed? I don't need this, she thought fiercely. She was shocked by the strong emotion that shook her. He could choose his own bedfellows. It was none of her business. But it was her bed.

She felt a hollowness inside, a pulsing, radiating ache as she realised for the first time since Peter's abrupt departure that she actually missed the comfort of a man's arms and a warmly sleeping body beside her. Though Peter's body had not always been warm, nor his arms comforting as he took his love elsewhere. She thought she had been managing pretty well without either. The arrival of Jonathan Howard had stirred all her dormant feelings and reminded her of what she had lost.

The cottage door was open, but Troy had to lean heavily against it for a moment to regain her composure. On the floor were some grocery boxes, packed with her kitchen goods. She did not know whether to be angry that she was being packed off so fast or pleased that he was helping with the chore. They would have to stay parked on the kitchen floor. It would take

Joe at least two days to clear out the lab flat and paint it, and she was not setting a foot inside until it was done.

She walked through the sitting-room feeling like an intruder. The room had an old stone fireplace which she had filled with dried flowers. The chintz-covered settee was strewn with cushions and magazines as she had left it last night; the long, polished window-seat heralded another glorious sea view. She had curled up there so many times, the endlessly changing sea soothing her nerves. She was going to miss all this so much.

Outside in the tiny garden she saw a recumbent figure under the whitebeam — in her deck-chair. She was about to stalk out and demand her chair back when she saw Jonathan's face. Although it was relaxed in sleep, the blue shadows under his eyes were like faint bruises and the pain lines from nose to mouth were clearly etched. It was, for a man, a classical face, with planes and contours so completely masculine, his dark hair falling across a high, intelligent forehead. She was not ready to cope with such a man. Perhaps never.

She could not understand why he disturbed her so. His only vice was that he had arrived two days too early. He was not responsible for his injuries. He could not help having an over-anxious elder sister. And Grace had good reason to be concerned about his convalescence. Skilled orthopaedic surgeons were in short supply. People were waiting in pain for their hip and knee replacements.

She went thoughtfully back into the kitchen. She would at least make the man a coffee. It would be her one and only olive-branch. She resolved to keep out of

Jonathan Howard's way until the three months were over.

He had left the kitchen cupboards bare. Troy replaced her tea and coffee, put the milk back in the refrigerator, and opened a packet of chocolate digestive biscuits. When the kettle had boiled, she made two steaming mugs of coffee and took them out into the garden with the biscuits on an odd-shaped plate. She collected a cushion as she went through the sitting-room.

Jonathan stirred and stretched as she sat down on the grass beside him.

'Coffee?' she asked, knowing that most surgeons were addicted to strong coffee.

'Thanks,' he said, taking a mug. 'Is this a peace-offering?'

'No, I'd do the same for any patient. Who's been looking after you since your accident?'

'I have a housekeeper at my house in London, but her sister is unwell and so I've let her go for an indefinite time. I've been managing on my own. I actually enjoy cooking.'

But not with those hands, thought Troy. They couldn't hold a tin-opener, let alone a saucepan. She imagined him living on a diet of sandwiches, takeaways and restaurant food.

'You'll eat with Grace now, of course,' said Troy. 'The school food is very good. We have an excellent cook.'

'No tapioca pudding?'

'It's served with stewed fruit these days. We have a

lot of diet-conscious young ladies. If it was all stodge, they'd just leave it.'

He took a couple of biscuits. 'What an unusual plate.'

Troy agreed with a smile. 'An experiment from the pottery classes. Why should all plates be round? Why not a triangular plate? Thank you for packing up the kitchen things. I can't take any of it till the flat's ready.'

'You're starting to make me feel awful,' he said laconically, looking nothing of the sort. The caffeine had pumped straight into his veins and he was revitalised. Troy realised how strong he was, despite his injuries.

'Good,' said Troy with spirit. 'I'm glad you feel awful. I'm being turned out of my home for the. . .' She almost said, Second time. The undersides of the leaves of the whitebeam were all silvery in the growing gloom of the evening, shimmering in the lowering rays of the sun. The painful blue of the sea reminded her of what she was about to lose.

'For no good reason,' she added lamely. 'However, since you're here, I hope you'll recognise that I'm in charge of the medical health of these girls and that there is no need for any interference on your part. The school medical scene is totally different from a big surgical hospital. They're a million miles apart. Although your knowledge is, of course, streets ahead of mine, I doubt if you have any actual experience of the medical requirements of eleven- to eighteen-year-olds. They rarely need hip replacements.'

'I do accept your concern,' said Jonathan smoothly. 'I shall not step on your toes, Troy. But don't turn your back on what could be useful back-up. A second opinion has its advantages in some circumstances.'

'I will remember that. But it's quite clear, isn't it, that I'm in charge of the medical centre?'

'I promise I won't interfere.'

She did not believe him. He was a medical man, dedicated, itching to be back at the helm, hands or no hands. He would not be able to keep away. She was going to have all sorts of problems.

'Come and have coffee any time,' he went on. 'Grace lent me the cottage, but she said nothing about the garden. You could consider that the garden is still yours.'

'And the whitebeam...' breathed Troy, the white petals falling on the grass around them as the wind stirred the branches. 'I'd like that, Mr Howard.'

'My friends call me Jonathan,' he said. 'Do you think you could try? Or do you prefer B. J.?'

'Just while you're here,' she said, knowing she was floundering. His presence blotted out everything. It was all she could do not to touch his hands, tell him that they would be all right soon, that they would heal naturally, and that he would be a great surgeon again.

'Who looks after your patients at night?'

'There's a part-time night nurse, Karen Norwood. She's very good and reliable. We get on very well when we see each other. She stands in on my day off, too, otherwise I would never get away.'

'And what do you do on your day off?'

'Walk everywhere. Walk the coastal paths, high moor, the cliffs and the sea-shore. It's very beautiful walking-country around here, with the hills and the river valley. I love it. It's so quiet and the coast is wonderful. I never tire of watching the sea.'

'I know that if I were in love with someone I should never tire of watching them, of looking at them, seeing the changing expressions on their face.'

He brushed a crumb from his mouth and Troy took her gaze away from its moist curve. She had never felt this kind of hunger for any man. Not even Peter. Her romance with him had been conventional, growing in feeling, not this sudden surge of desire.

A soft pencilling of light hid his face. It was impossible to tell if he was serious or merely mocking her. Troy decided he was mocking her, taking a rise, seeing how she would react.

'Beware of changing expressions,' she said lightly. 'You may never know what is causing those emotions. Observation is always part diagnostic.'

She finished her coffee and stood up. She did not want to walk back in the dark, although she knew every inch of the school grounds. She was not afraid of the dark, of bats or owls. She often saw hedgehogs at night and put a little meat out for them. It was always gone in the morning, the saucer licked clean.

'I'll leave you to settle in, Jonathan,' she said, 'while I do my own settling. Though I suppose your sister's spare room is only transitory. My own darling little attic will be ready in a couple of days. I can't wait to move in.'

'I do apologise. . .' he began again.

'Is that your apology face?' she said suddenly. It was something she often said to little girls when they said they were sorry. It always made them laugh. 'Is that your sorry face?' she would say to a woebegone little girl. Laughter went a long way when a child was frightened.

His expression relaxed. His laugh was rich and deep, a sound which touched her heart. She hated him for making himself so appealing. She did not want to like him or anything about him. He had taken her home from her. He would interfere at the medical centre, undermine her authority. He was altogether an unwelcome visitor to Belling Hills.

'I'll walk you back to the school,' he said, standing up and unfolding his long legs from the deck-chair. He extended his hand to take the tray, but she was already on her way into the cottage.

'No need,' she said cheerily. 'I know the way blindfolded. It's not late and it's not dark.'

He turned back his cuff and looked at his watch. 'I'm having supper with Grace in half an hour. I might as well go your way. It's no trouble.'

They both heard the calls at the same time, faint but with a distinct edge of urgency. They looked at each other.

'Did you hear that?'

'It seems to be coming from below, from the beach.'

'Don't go near the edge,' Troy warned. 'There hasn't been a landslide for fifty years, but it's very treacherous. We can take a quick path down to the beach from the end of the lane.'

They heard the cries again and moved at speed through the cottage and along the lane to where it petered out into a rough slope that was just about climbable.

'Call this a path?' Jonathan grumbled as he scrambled down after Troy.

'It's a darned sight quicker than walking over the cliffs to the estuary,' said Troy between drawing breath. 'I can see them. Look, two youngsters over there, by the water's edge. One of them seems to be in trouble.'

A boy was sprawled on the silvery sand. His friend was shaking him, calling for help, his whole body distraught and shaking. He caught sight of Troy and Jonathan and waved them over frantically.

'It's my mate,' he cried. 'He went under the waves. He's not breathing. Do something. Do something. . .'

Jonathan was on his knees immediately, his head on the boy's wet chest. Both boys were about fourteen, in fluorescent swimming shorts. Troy saw some beer cans by the boys' towels on the beach.

'Tell us exactly what happened,' said Troy.

'We were going for a swim when this big wave knocked Jimmy over. He went under. I thought he would come up again, but he didn't. Then I saw him and I pulled him out. . .' The boy's face was pinched with shock, white round the nostrils.

'You did very well,' said Troy, trying to comfort him. She handed him a towel. 'Dry yourself now. We'll see to your friend.'

'He's not breathing,' said Jonathan. Around them the waves were crested with foaming surf whipped up by a fresh wind. He looked up at Troy quickly, his hair blowing in all directions. 'We've got to work fast.'

Jonathan detected a faint pulse in the boy's neck and he began clearing the airways and pumping water from the boy's lungs. Troy supported the back of the neck and tipped the boy's head well back. The surgeon pinched the boy's nose and began mouth-to-mouth resuscitation, blowing strongly into his lungs four times. He gave a breath every five seconds, stopping to listen for air leaving the lungs, and watching the chest wall.

It was relentless and tiring, but Troy knew they must continue for at least twenty minutes to get the lungs functioning again. People had been known to recover after even longer periods of mouth-to-mouth.

She was beginning to get cramp and eased her position slightly. Their heads were close as they worked on the boy. Troy was immensely aware of this closeness and for a second she wondered what it would be like to be held in his arms. She knew she would be fighting her good sense. For the same second her concentration wavered.

'Sister,' he rasped, as he came up for air.

'Cramp,' she said.

Suddenly Jimmy choked and spluttered and drew in a shallow breath. In moments he was breathing normally. Troy sat back on her heels.

'Thank goodness,' she whispered.

They turned him and put him into the recovery position. There were no obvious injuries. Jonathan was phoning for an ambulance, using his cordless telephone. He would have one, thought Troy, turning her attention to the other boy, who was clearly upset.

'Jimmy's going to be all right,' she told him. 'He's breathing on his own now and an ambulance will be here soon. What's your name and where do you both live?'

It was half an hour before the ambulance men appeared, trudging over the shingle with a stretcher. Troy had kept Jimmy warm with his own clothes and Jonathan's jacket, rubbing the boy's hands and feet. The light had almost gone and the beach was an eerie place in the dark, the waves breaking on the shore with almost sinister regularity.

Jonathan was quiet and withdrawn, not as elated as most doctors would have been.

'Aren't you pleased?' she asked. 'You saved his life. A young boy. He's got a future now.'

Jonathan was staring down at his hands as if they disgusted him. She could see the pain on his face, etched in the darkening of his eyes and furrowed brow.

'Saved him? Yes, I suppose I did, because I happen to be capable of blowing oxygen into his lungs. Anyone could have done it. But what about the long waiting-lists? There are so many patients, young and old, who have little or no future beyond pain and immobility and all because of me, because of my hands. How can I hold a screw fixator, a bridging device, marker pins? What use is a surgeon who can't hold a knife steady?'

Troy was stunned by the anger in his voice. He was blaming himself, hostile to the world and to the fate that had conspired to bring him down and let his immense talent go to waste. Leaving her home for three months was bad enough; to have this awkward man on her doorstep was going to be very difficult. But she understood his agony and she did not want to understand him. She wanted nothing to do with him at all. He was like a brewing storm, a warning on the horizon. Dark clouds were gathering over her head and she had nowhere to run for shelter.

CHAPTER THREE

TROY needed a bracing dose of fresh sea air to blow away all the aggravation of the last few days. As she made plans for her day off, she tried to shut her mind to Jonathan's presence at the school. He always seemed to be around, his tall figure commanding and purposeful, stopping to talk to someone or admire a view. He did not seem to be settling to his work.

She fancied a walk along the waterfront at Salcombe and then a climb up to Bolt Head. The views were rocky and spectacular. But it would have to wait till she had transport.

She changed into a maize-coloured cotton tracksuit and trainers and tied her hair back with a silk scarf. The coastal path near Belling Hills was not steep enough to need her walking boots. The narrow, sunken lane from the school to the cliff path was deserted, the hedges thick with wild flowers, the bearded clematis sweet-smelling, lupins glowing with colour.

It was one of her favourite walks along the rugged cliff, part of it dropping sheer to the sea, the rest with rolling pastures sloping gently from path to cove. In places the cliff had slid away, and red flags warned walkers not to go near the edge. Butterflies fluttered like confetti among the pinky sea-thrift.

A kestrel hovered in the air, wings barely moving, suddenly darting down to the bracken. Troy watched, fascinated by its skill. Vaguely she heard a disturbing sound. It was music, growing louder. She recognised a melody from one of London's top musicals.

'Oh, no,' she breathed as she saw a dark-haired walker ahead stop and turn round with a mocking salute. She marshalled her thoughts in readiness.

'You're looking disapprovingly at me,' said Jonathan. 'What country code have I broken now? Am I supposed to walk this path clockwise or anticlockwise?'

'You can walk it standing on your head if you want to. But this isn't London,' Troy said, with a nod towards the small portable compact-disc player in his hand. 'It doesn't matter how much noise you make there — take a brass band — but not here, please. The peace and quiet of the countryside is for everyone.'

He switched it off and put the player in the back pocket of his well cut navy trousers. 'Of course, I do agree. It's just that I don't always like my own company, nor my own thoughts. They're somewhat painful. But now that I have you for conversation, then the music won't be needed.'

'Don't bank on it,' she said, overtaking. 'I'm a fast walker and I don't intend to amble along. I don't suppose you're used to walking, being a Londoner with a car and taxis to take you everywhere.'

'I jog and swim regularly,' he said, falling into an easy stride with her, ignoring her attempts to shake him off. 'Apart from my hands, I'm fit enough to keep up with you.'

'There's some steep hills around here,' she said,

determined to discourage him. 'They take stamina. You may not be able to make them.'

'But not along this stretch,' he said. 'It's fairly moderate. I checked the map contours before I came out. Just a few pleasant ups and downs, all within normal ability.'

'It's your choice,' she said, swallowing her annoyance. 'You should know how fit you feel.'

They walked in silence, Troy trying to take her usual pleasure from the sweeping panoramic scenery but acutely conscious of the man at her side. His long legs were matching her stride, his hair blowing in the wind, tailored shirt flapping. She could not meet the irony in his eyes, knowing that they were probably laughing at her.

'How are you settling into your new flat at the school?' he asked with the tact of a raving rhinoceros in a flowerbed. 'Fitting in all right?'

'Fitting in? Are you joking? To say that it's small is an understatement,' she said, gritting her teeth. 'I can't even unpack. My books will have to stay boxed, my clothes are hanging round the picture frame like washing, and anything surplus to the day's requirements is still on the landing outside.'

'That's tough,' he said, sounding genuinely sympathetic. 'Then you can see how hopeless it would have been for me. I would have got claustrophobia, had to sleep with my feet out of the window.'

'What about my feet? My claustrophobia? The cottage is small, but at least there are four good rooms and a garden. Now I have to get out as much as I can before I start banging my head on the walls.'

'My offer about the garden still stands. Why don't you come and have coffee, read, sunbathe — do whatever nurses do in their spare time. Don't wait for an invitation. You haven't been down once.'

'I haven't had time; besides, I think I would find it upsetting, being a visitor in my own home.'

'It's a pity you feel like that, but I should remind you that the cottage is not exactly your own home. It belongs to the school. It goes with the job, I understand from Grace.'

'Of course, you're absolutely right. I'm so glad you have all the facts.' Troy's resentment was hard to keep under control. 'I don't own the cottage, nor ever will, but it still feels like home to me. I've lived there a year and it's the nearest to a home I've had for a long time.'

'Where have you been living? Surely most nurses share a flat or something?'

'I lived in residence at the hospital,' she said briefly, not wanting to remember or talk about when she'd lost her home. She had put so much of herself into that house — painting, decorating, sewing. It had been like leaving a second skin behind. 'In another poky room. It was more convenient for my work. Less hassle.'

They stopped as they reached the top of the hill; the view took Troy's breath away. They stood in splendid isolation, their disagreement wiped away by the endless, sparkling indigo-blue of the sea and the rolling green of the rocky headland in the distance. Powerful waves pounded great slabs of rock standing like black monoliths, spilling crests of white over the glistening smoothness.

'How come the rocks are so smooth, cut like slabs of chocolate cake?' he asked, genuinely interested.

'I think the rocks are called mica-schist slabs, fractured into flat pieces. In some earth movement they were overturned and folded into these complex formations.'

'Quite the little geologist, aren't you?' But the remark was teasing, not mocking. Troy turned her face to the sun, eyes half closed.

Jonathan was staring out to sea, lost in his own thoughts, his rugged profile and angular jaw etched against the sky like a modern Raleigh. Troy was aware of her nerve-ends tingling as she stood beside him. She had forgotten what it was like to be so aware of a man, so much so that she had to dig her hands into her pockets to stop herself from touching his arm.

The memory of her husband was like an unwanted shadow in the background. Had she really been married to Peter? Sometimes it felt as if it had all happened to someone else and she had merely been a bemused spectator. It surprised her that she should have almost forgotten him, a man who had hurt her so badly. The man had gone, but the hurt lingered. Perhaps there was some chance of a normal life with someone one day, some kind and strong man who would love her and share a life with her. But did such a man exist and wouldn't he be hard to find? Weren't they all untrustworthy. . .?

A sly wind caught the ends of her silk scarf and it slid from her hair. She reached out to grab the streamer as it flew by, long hair blinding her for a moment. Everything went out of focus as she swung round.

Jonathan's hands grasped her arm, pulling her back and hard against him, his elbows digging into her sides as his hands lost their grip. It was the second time she had felt those muscles and the solid wall of Jonathan's chest.

'You little fool! What are you trying to do? Kill yourself for a scarf?' His voice was taut with anger.

The warmth of his bare arms was disturbing against her skin as she struggled to regain a proper footing. He held her close, moulding her body to his, refusing to let her move. It all happened so quickly. She knew she had been foolish.

'It was instinctive,' she gasped. 'I didn't realise how close I was. . .'

Troy tried to extract herself from his grasp. It was insufferable that he should still be holding her. The danger was over. The scarf was now a thin wisp of white nearing the surface of the waves like a moth going to its doom.

'Is this instinctive, too?' he asked, his mouth finding her lips with tentative gentleness. She tried to push him away with a small, shocked cry, but his arms were like iron. The kiss deepened and she felt her resistance fading as a kind of hunger took over. Troy was held captive in the warmth of his embrace. They were both lost in a kiss that went on and on, the sea wind buffeting their bodies, the sound of the waves overwhelming the pounding of their hearts.

'I think this is a little stupid,' she managed to say at last, breaking away awkwardly. 'We're not over-sexed teenagers. . .'

'Definitely not. Sex-starved, perhaps, but not over-sexed. Excessively stupid,' he agreed huskily, his piercing blue eyes drinking in the lovely wind-swept woman in his arms. His feelings were in a turmoil. He felt alive for the first time in months, but warning bells were sounding. He had to keep this light, very light. 'But very good therapy for patients recovering from helicopter accidents. Would you recommend three times a day, after meals, Sister?'

Troy would have laughed if she had not been so dismayed at her reaction. 'Danger of overdosing when it's a long, hot summer, Doctor,' she said. 'Has Grace told you to soft soap me so that I'll stay on? The school needs me. The parents like to know that their daughters are being properly cared for, that their health is not in amateur hands.'

'Soft soap you?' Jonathan scoffed. 'I wouldn't have the temerity. I kissed you because I wanted to kiss you, no ulterior motive. A perfectly normal reaction to being with a pretty girl.'

'Mind you don't slip on the suds,' said Troy, beginning to walk on, heading downwards now towards the silvery river estuary snaking inland. 'It has all the hallmarks of a calculated move to keep Sister Kingsbury sweet. Kisses being handed out with a pat on the head for being a good girl.'

She heard his sharp intake of breath behind her on the narrow path as he bit back an exclamation, and the cracking sound as he stamped on some dry bracken. She knew it was not true, but the words were out before she could stop them.

'I would not have described my behaviour as offensive, nor did I think it was all that revolting for you.

Really, you had me fooled, Sister. I guess my kissing is out of practice. I'll make sure I don't make the same mistake again. Be assured I won't come within firing distance.'

'Good. That's how I prefer it. The less I see of you the better. Leave me to get on with my work and you can get on with yours, whatever you say it is.'

'I have a paper to write for the *British Medical Journal* on big and small bone disease.'

'Then I'm sure they're waiting for it with bated breath. Stop the presses and hold the front page.' Her sensitive antennae told her that she had gone more than far enough for the time being. It was like walking with a ticking time bomb tied to her heels.

'Naturally they are,' he said, rubbing his fingers, some of his good humour returning now they had changed the topic. 'But I can't understand the keyboard, the command keys. It's defeating me.'

'Pity. It's the best possible physio for your fingers. Typing and playing the piano. You should do some repetitive exercises every day.'

'I need to be taught. I have no idea how that monstrous bag of tricks works, and the handbook is written in a foreign language.'

'It looks difficult, but not once you get the hang of it. . . Even our eleven-year-olds can use a computer.'

'The brain is rather less accommodating at thirty-eight. Will you show me how it works? You're using the same model in the medical centre.'

She recoiled from the commanding tone, the arrogant shrug of his shoulders. He seemed to think he had the right to ask her to do anything.

'Am I hearing you correctly?' she said with suppressed annoyance. 'First you take over my cottage for your own use. You expect me to drive you to Totnes for your physiotherapy. And now you want me to give you lessons in using a word processor. Perhaps you'd like me to do your laundry. Shall I come and wash your socks?'

He did not acknowledge her question. 'It wouldn't take long, Troy,' he said. 'As you say, once I get the hang of it. . .'

She felt trapped by his persuasiveness. She was just about to quicken her step as the path led down towards the sand-dunes and the estuary when she caught sight of a girl in the distinctive mauve Belling Hills uniform. The girl was running across the dunes, red hair flying, stumbling as her feet found the soft sand.

'That's Lucy Warren,' said Troy under her breath. 'What on earth is she doing out here?'

Jonathan caught her up, following her gaze. 'Isn't that a Belling girl? Shouldn't she be in class?'

'Yes, I'm going down to her. It's Lucy Warren, a quiet youngster. I recognise that hair. She hardly speaks to anyone.'

They hurried down the cliff path, climbing the stile that lead to the sand. A hedge of brambles hid them from the shelving dunes. They caught sight of Lucy's red hair again.

'She's making for the headland at the south end of the sands. I hope she's not going swimming. It can be dangerous there. All the red flags are up.'

'Let's hurry.'

They began to run, slipping and sliding on the slopes.

Troy was worried and drew a steadying breath. Splintered fragments of brilliance bounced off the sea. It looked so deceptive. Lucy might easily think it was safe.

'Don't be alarmed,' he added, touching her arm with swift reassurance. 'We'll find her in time.'

Jonathan had known what she was thinking. She was torn by this unexpected support, knowing it was something she had never experienced before. Yet she would not allow him to break down her defences. She refused to be at his beck and call.

'There she is! Among the grass.'

Lucy was crouched among the long grass, rocking on her heels. There was an apple and a book beside her. She did not look as if she was going swimming.

'Lucy! Lucy, whatever are you doing down here? Shouldn't you be in class?' Troy went down on her knees by the girl. Lucy's face went pale.

'Sister Kingsbury,' she trembled, moistening her lips. 'Please don't be cross with me.' She looked desperately from Troy to Jonathan. 'I'm not doing any harm.'

'I'm not angry with you, Lucy. I'm only concerned that you're wandering about on your own instead of being in class. It's not like you to be playing truant. Surely your teacher will miss you?'

'I said I had a headache. . .'

'And have you?' Troy remembered that Lucy had been to the medical centre one evening with a headache. She had not returned the next day so Troy had presumed that it had gone.

'And I was tired.'

'But you were planning to read,' said Troy, noticing

the book. 'It's not easy to read with a headache. It usually hurts the eyes too much.'

'I thought my headache might get better by the sea.' The girl looked away, the corners of her mouth turned down. 'Are you going to report me?'

'I'll think about it,' said Troy. 'Let's go back to the school now before you're in real trouble.' She looked up at Jonathan, who at least had the sense not to interfere in this situation. 'No need for you to abandon your walk, Mr Howard. The river estuary is really lovely further along and there are fords where you can walk across the water when the tide's out. Or perhaps you don't need any fords. I'll go back with Lucy.'

'You could be right,' he said. 'Any good pubs along the way for lunch?'

'Tired of school food already?' she said. 'You'll find several nice old inns with perfect views and excellent food.'

'I'm sorry you won't be joining me,' he said, with glinting eyes. He had been watching her closely as she dealt with Lucy. 'We could have continued our conversation.'

'Conversation? I'll bring a script with me next time,' she said lightly, more for Lucy's benefit. 'Still, I'm glad you're sorry. It terminates our enforced walk on a more suitable note.' She helped Lucy up on to her feet. 'Come along, young lady. We'd better walk pretty fast.'

She heard a deep chuckle as she turned Lucy away from the sea. She did not bother to look. She could imagine the amused expression on that man's face.

What a wonderful way to spend her day off, thought

Troy as they climbed back over the sand-dunes. Lucy had come across the fields and farmland, trespassing, which was quicker than the coastal path. Troy decided to take a chance, keeping an eye open for any of the marked public paths.

They did not meet any irate farmers or equally irate bulls. As they neared the school, Troy decided what she should do about Lucy. The girl ought to be reported, but Troy did not see how this course would help. It was not discipline she needed, but some kind of counselling.

'Let's go straight to the medical centre,' said Troy, 'and I'll give you something for your headache. Then I suggest that you go on to your next class. I shall say nothing about finding you on the dunes, but if you've been missed by your teacher and I'm asked I shall tell the truth. And I hope you will too. Of course, they may think you've been lying down on your bed.'

'Thank you, Sister. I'm sorry to have ruined your walk.'

'It doesn't matter. I wasn't really enjoying it.'

There was something odd about the girl, but Troy could not pin it down. Lucy did not run from her as any other thirteen-year-old might. She walked in a watchful, nervous way as if she did not want to be noticed. Yet she had been running on the sand, finding a kind of freedom there.

It was too late to salvage much of her day off. Troy decided to have a swim in the school pool, then eat her packed lunch in a secluded cove with a good book and the seagulls for company. She knew lots of places, smugglers' coves of long ago.

The swim was refreshing and she had the pool to herself. She concentrated on improving her crawl stroke and hoped all thoughts of Jonathan would vanish. Lydia Richmond had been giving her some coaching.

'Bend the arm high, thumb in first, brush past thigh,' she intoned mentally.

He was just an attractive man and she had momentarily been taken in by his good looks. It was nothing more than that. It could happen to anyone, especially to a woman who had not been kissed for a long time, a woman who was beached at Belling Hills like a small, lonely whale.

That was it, she decided, smiling to herself, a lack of love creating a certain hunger which had made her vulnerable, even weak. It was nothing to be ashamed of. . . But that kiss. . . It had been magic. But she would make sure it did not happen again. She did not want Jonathan to think that she went with the cottage.

She lost her breathing concentration and swallowed a mouthful of water. No more Jonathan Howard. She cemented the dent in her heart which would prevent any repetition of those glorious moments on the clifftop.

By the time she reached the sandy cove where they had saved Jimmy, she was feeling more in control of the situation. She shook out her wet hair and settled herself against a convenient rock, a rolled towel cushioning her shoulders. She had filled a roll with cottage cheese, walnuts, iceberg lettuce and sliced tomato. It was bulging with goodness.

The sun, the food and the book made her relax, and

drowsiness crept over her without warning. She was not sleeping well in the little bedroom in the attic flat and it was catching up on her.

She woke suddenly, blinking against the sun in her eyes, to see a pair of male legs in black knee-length latex swimming-trunks standing not far away.

'For heaven's sake, can't you leave me alone to enjoy a nap on my day off?' she murmured.

'I'm most terribly sorry, Sister Kingsbury. I didn't mean to disturb you. I only came ashore on my surfer and thought it was you. You were reading. . .'

Troy came to with a jolt. She recognised that hesistant, apologetic voice and realised that the legs belonged to a much shorter man than Jonathan Howard. She saw the windsurfing sail fanned on the beach like a wet dragonfly and knew it was Dr Roger Wright, the GP from the clinic.

She sat up quickly, the open book falling on to the sand. 'I didn't realise it was you, Dr Wright. I thought it was someone else. You've been windsurfing?'

He grinned boyishly, fair hair flopping over his forehead. 'Yes, lovely day for it. Nice fresh wind. Have you ever tried it, Sister Kingsbury?'

She shook her head. 'Never. Remember, I'm basically a green Londoner. I'm only just getting used to fresh air. I don't think I could keep my balance. I doubt if I could even stand up.'

'Like everything else, it takes practice. I could teach you if you'd like to learn.'

'That's very kind, and I'll remember if I find enough courage. And there's no need to call me Sister

Kingsbury when we're not at the medical centre. On a deserted beach you could call me Troy.'

Roger flushed with pleasure and Troy's eyes softened. She was dealing with an easily pleased young man and must be careful not to give him ideas. It would be very unfair.

'I'd like that, Troy,' he said, picking up her book. 'You're so easy to talk to. I feel as if I've known you for ages.'

'You have known me for ages, at least a year,' said Troy, trying to sound brisk and practical. 'You're very good at Belling Hills. We all appreciate the interest you take, and the girls like and trust you. That's important. So much depends on a school's relationship with the local GPs.'

'And the school's co-operation,' said Roger, obviously set to linger. 'You're a reliable diagnostician and never call us out in a panic.'

Troy smiled her thanks for the compliment. She did not want to encourage the young doctor. She had a good book and wanted to read now that she had woken up. It seemed that the entire medical profession was in league to ruin her day off. 'Don't speak too soon. I may yet call you out in the middle of the night for a girl who's been on a chocolate binge.'

'I shan't mind,' he said confidentially. 'As long as you continue making that excellent coffee. You always have my favourite biscuits.'

Troy's mind went blank. His favourite biscuits? What on earth could they be? 'That's a promise, then.'

'Don't forget my offer about windsurfing. Any time. . .' He hesitated. Troy sensed that he was getting up his courage to ask her out, and she did not want to have to say no. She hurriedly got up and brushed the browny-pink sand off her tracksuit, looking at her watch. But it was not on her wrist. She remembered taking it off before swimming. It would be at the pool.

'How kind. Hadn't you better get back into the water? You'll get chilled, standing there wet.'

'Not me. I'm immune to colds, chills, flu, German measles. You name it and I won't get it.'

Troy laughed. He was easy company. He waved as he dragged his surfer into the sea, wading into the capricious waves. He leaped on to the thin float and expertly caught the wind in his sails. In seconds he was skimming out to sea, no longer a bedraggled dragonfly but a splash of bright colour. Troy was glad he was good at something. Everyone needed to have an achievement. She decided she did not have one.

But there was no way she was going to encourage this young man, even though he was pleasant company. He would take it seriously and in no time be planting ownership stakes around her, and that was the last thing she wanted. She did not want to belong to anyone.

She wandered back along the lanes to the school, strangely at a loose end. If she had been in her cottage, there would have been chores to do. The school laundry was washing her linen and uniform while she was in the attic flat. She had enjoyed gardening, her plants perched high above the sea like divers ready to take the plunge. Then she would have spent the cooling twilight hours with a glass of wine in the garden, listening to music or reading. All of those simple pleasures were denied her now because of Jonathan Howard. Grace's hospitality to her brother was understandable, but it was hard to take.

So why not? Why not go and sit in the cottage garden as he had suggested more than once? It was only the cottage she had had to give up. She turned towards the low-roofed stone dwelling, rehearsing what she would say if she saw him. He might have walked further round the estuary, hopefully got lost, and she would have the garden to herself.

'Hello, tree,' she said to the whitebeam as she let herself in round the side. 'I hope you're keeping him awake. Bang on the window really hard.'

She heard a slight cough as Jonathan came out of the cottage, glass in hand. 'How quaint, Troy, talking to trees? I would not have suspected you of having a touch of the HRHs.'

'I like this tree,' she said, refusing to be riled. She put an arm round the hard wood of its slender trunk. 'It's my friend.'

'And we all need friends,' he said drily. 'Have you seen what's been delivered?'

'A mobile home?' she asked hopefully.

'It's round the front.'

'I came the other way.'

He took her arm and steered her in that direction. Troy tried to keep a distance, remembering the chemistry that had flared between them on the cliffs. She preferred not to be intimidated by his closeness. Outside the cottage was parked a gleaming navy Jaguar E-Type roadster. It was a beautiful car, at least thirty years old.

'Nice car,' Troy admitted, not letting on that she thought the car was a dream. Its long bonnet was low and powerful. 'A new toy for you?'

He ignored the remark, walking round the car with obvious pride.

'It's a classic. It has a 4.2-litre engine, manual gearbox, wire wheels you can see. I bought it just before my accident. I've hardly driven it.'

'I suppose we are looking at thirty-five thousand pounds?'

'Nearer forty thousand. They're hard to find.' He dropped the ignition keys into her hand. 'There, Troy, it's yours for the duration.' He made it sound like a war. 'I've taken out insurance to cover you. You can go wherever you like in it. No more having to get lifts from staff to take young ladies to the dentist. Regard the car as a swap for the cottage.'

The realisation washed over Troy with a *frisson* of excitement. It was a gesture of such generosity, and she was unused to such gestures. Peter had always taken, not given.

'I am grateful,' said Troy slowly, 'and appreciate the sentiment behind the loan of the car. But it doesn't make me feel any better about the cottage. Anyway, how do you know I'll be able to drive it? I might have an obsession with the Mini, or be a hopeless driver.'

'I don't believe Sister Kingsbury is hopeless at anything, except perhaps at falling in love.'

'Join half the population,' said Troy drily. 'I don't believe that's an area of my life of which you have any knowledge. I suppose you've left a trail of broken hearts and tear-drenched aprons throughout London's teaching hospitals.'

'Very few. Hardly any aprons,' he said, a veiled look turning his eyes to a glittering navy. 'I was married for several years and have a daughter. She lives with her grandmother in Wiltshire.'

There was a degree of bitterness in his voice which was unexpected. It took her by surprise. Even his garden was not full of roses. She might have known he would be married, but something had gone wrong. Taking a cue from the whereabouts of his daughter, it seemed that Mrs Howard was no longer around.

'You're very trusting with your precious old car,' she said, changing the subject swiftly. 'I could dent its ego just turning in this lane.'

'I don't think my judgement is at fault, nor is your eyesight. You have to trust people or nothing moves forward.'

'Ah, the penny drops,' said Troy thoughtfully. 'You want a lift to the hospital for your physio.'

'As it happens, I shall...but that's not what I meant...' he countered, biting his lip. 'Moving forward meant...oh, I don't know what I meant.'

'When do you want to go?'

'I haven't an appointment. I thought I should find out first when you're free.'

Troy heaved an exaggerated sigh. 'I'll take you in my lunch-break tomorrow if I can get you an appointment.'

'As efficient as ever,' he said. 'You'll let me know?'

'I certainly won't send you a postcard,' said Troy, turning on her heel. This man was so complacent about getting his own way every time. She added complacency and manipulativeness to his list of personal characteristics. The list was getting to be long and unattractive. But then she remembered that kiss and vowed to keep a tight rein on her rocketing emotions.

'Please think again about my offer of help at the medical centre,' he said. 'I'm sure we could work together. The cottage is pretty isolated and I feel at a loose end. After a bustling hospital, it's so quiet.'

'Coastguard cottages are quiet,' said Troy. 'That's why I love it so much. Just the wind and the sea and me.'

'I need to work,' he insisted. 'This life of leisure is alien. I'm used to working all hours, snatching sleep when I can. Now I seem to do nothing else but sleep.'

'Perhaps you need the sleep. The body heals itself when at rest. It's doing you good. Besides, my day is mostly cuts and bruises and nosebleeds. . .hardly stretching work for an orthopaedic surgeon.'

'There must be routine work I could take over for you. How about your health and hygiene classes? Couldn't I do some of them for you? You could give me a list of topics.'

'No, you can't do my classes for me,' said Troy coldly. The classes were her idea, her special time with the girls. He was certainly not going to take them over, oozing charm and forceful personality with every word. The girls would be crazy about him in five minutes, imagining themselves in love.

'But there's first aid,' she went on. 'I've been meaning to start first-aid classes ever since the tooth incident and the boy on the beach. The girls ought to know what to do in an emergency.'

Jonathan swallowed hard. She could see that this was a blow to his pride, but she had to admire the way he pulled himself together. 'I'll start practising splints right away,' he said.

CHAPTER FOUR

THE girl's voice rose to a wail. 'I can't do it. I can't do it,' she cried. 'I'll never be able to use the stupid thing.'

Troy looked out of the window towards the distant hills of Dartmoor. Patience, patience, she told herself. The moors were golden green, slashed with purple patches, calm and majestic from this distance, wild and desolate at close quarters. Wild ponies still roamed the moors and the shaggy black moorland cattle cropped the coarse grass.

'Of course you will, Drusilla,' said Troy calmly. 'It just takes practice to use the inhaler, and that's why you're here. Let's try it again slowly.'

Drusilla was the last of the morning's walking wounded with bruises, sprains, cuts and minor ailments. The girl had asthma and was having difficulty with her inhaler. Troy had noticed she was not using it properly.

'In, out, hold...that's better. Keep practising and don't panic. These inhalers do work and they do help. It'll pay you to get the hang of it. Everything will be much easier.'

'I can't breathe, I can't breathe,' Drusilla wheezed anxiously.

'Yes, you can,' said Troy. 'You're doing very well. Try again.' Drusilla had moderate asthma and only needed to use the disodium cromoglycate spinhaler three or four times a day. She was allergic to dust and the only thing they could do in class was to seat her well away from the blackboard. She had extra swimming time as this was the best form of sport for an asthmatic child.

Drusilla tossed back her long fair hair over her shoulders. Troy suppressed a smile. Another tosser. This age-group of girls was like a herd of Dartmoor ponies, always tossing their manes.

Troy tried not to hurry the girl. It had been a long surgery and she had a lot to do that morning before taking Jonathan for his physio treatment. Healthy-living classes were her pet idea and they were popular with the pupils, probably because they did not involve any written work. The last thing Troy wanted was a pile of essays to mark.

'But I think you should set an end-of-term examination paper,' Grace had said recently. 'It would be interesting to know how much the girls have taken in.'

Troy agreed reluctantly. It meant she would have to find time to mark the papers. 'About ten per cent. Diet and haircare are their top priorities.'

'Jonathan could help you mark the papers,' Grace suggested, unconsciously reading Troy's mind. 'After all, he is used to students, being an examiner at the Royal College of Surgery.'

Troy tried to find a tactful answer. She had had enough of Jonathan's high achievements. He was so good at everything. She did not want him interfering in her classes; in no time they would be arguing over personal hygiene or contraception methods.

'I'm sure Jonathan will be far too busy writing his paper on bones,' said Troy smoothly. 'I'll manage.'

Her classes went well. The girls enjoyed them and the entertaining way she put over the information. They were all keenly interested in their appearance and it had dawned on them that health and hygiene went hand in hand with an attractive body.

Troy raced up to her flat and changed out of her uniform into flowered jeans and a big loose T-shirt, tying her hair back with a matching bandeau. She was not going to dress up for a car. She grabbed her bag and made sure she had some money. While Jonathan was having his physio, she would take a rare opportunity to look at the shops.

He was waiting for her, leaning on the car, the roof already down, mentally tapping his watch. 'You're late.'

'A hundred lines?' she said, not mentioning the classes in case Grace had already broached the subject of the exams. '"I mustn't mislay my watch"? Or how about "I mustn't keep sir waiting"?'

'How careless. A nurse without a watch. Unthinkable.'

She bit back a retort and got into the driving-seat. This was not the time for a heated exchange. She switched on the engine and waited for Jonathan to get in. He poured himself over the top of the door without opening it.

'I've always wanted to do that,' he grinned.

The boyish remark relaxed her immediately. Perhaps it was meant to. She drove the car apprehensively for the first few miles along the narrow lanes, praying she would not meet a coach coming the other way and have to reverse to a passing-point. The Jaguar responded beautifully and her confidence grew.

'You're handling the car well,' said Jonathan.

'I used to drive a BMW,' she said.

'Did you? When?'

'Oh. . .some time ago. When my life was different.'

'Down on your luck now, are you?'

'You could say that. A forced change of circumstances.'

'We could talk about it if it helps.'

'No, thank you,' she said primly. 'Talking doesn't help. I'm managing to put that period of my life behind me. I'm blocking it out. I don't want to remember anything. It's better buried and forgotten.'

'How wise you are, Sister Kingsbury. Everyone should bury their ghosts. They are not good company.'

Troy took a darting look at him. His face was a mask. Were his hands his sole injury or was there more, much more? He was staring intently at the winding road ahead, jaw set in a determined line. He did not look like a man who could be disturbed by ghosts.

She parked the car neatly in an area outside the hospital. 'I'll be back in an hour,' she said. 'I've a few errands.'

She was not going to nursemaid him through his appointment. He was quite capable of coping on his own. He could practise being charming and affable to the medical staff.

There was not enough time to walk the ramparts or look round the circular shell keep of the ruined castle which dominated the town of Totnes. Instead she strolled the picturesque streets and Butterwalk, the two bridges that straddled the River Dart. Totnes had once been a port of some importance, with a history that went back to Roman times.

Nor was there time for Troy to see the historic Brutus Stone set in a pavement near the fifteenth-century East Gate. Another time, she told herself, as she hurriedly bought some flowers to brighten the flat. The big bunch of marigolds and sweet peas cheered her as she hurried back to the hospital.

Jonathan was waiting, but not impatiently. He looked more relaxed, perhaps feeling at home in a hospital environment once again. An expensive girls' boarding-school was alien territory. He caught sight of Troy and walked towards her, producing paper-wrapped cornflowers from behind his back. He had bought them in the hospital shop.

'Snap,' he said, offering them to her.

Troy took the flowers, momentarily off balance. She was startlingly aware of the authority he had relinquished, the brownness of the capable hands that had lost their power and skill. She felt a surge of pity for the man; it was suddenly right that she should be helping him.

'How kind,' she said. 'The flat does need plenty of cheering up. As I do.'

'How about some lunch?' he was saying. 'More cheering up.'

She shook her head. 'I have to get back. This is my lunch hour. I'm due back on duty.'

'You ought to eat. It's hardly sensible to go without food.'

'No problem; I'll get a sandwich from the kitchens.'

'It won't take ten minutes. How about that coffee-shop over there? It looks friendly. I want to tell you about my physiotherapy.'

'You could tell me in the car.'

He took no notice of her objections and was steering her through the door into the café, choosing a polished wood table by the window and calling over a waitress. There was no way of shifting Jonathan. He was determined to eat first. Troy was trapped.

'A toasted cheese and mushroom sandwich,' she ordered after a brief glance at the menu. 'And coffee, please.'

'Steak sandwich,' he ordered. 'Apple pie and cream. Coffee.'

Troy found she was hungry and she ate with haste. She wanted to get back to the school. Jonathan took his time, describing his treatment in detail. Troy tried to take an interest, but all the while she was aware of time passing, looking out of habit at her non-existent watch.

At last they were back in the car, and Troy drove as fast as the narrowness of the lanes allowed. She had a gut feeling that she ought to be at Belling Hills. She was sure something had happened. She almost took a racing turn into the drive to the school, roaring up to the medical centre. A small group of girls was waiting in the courtyard. They looked anxious. One of the girls ran up to the car as Troy pulled on the brakes.

'Sister! Sister! It's Ellen. She's been hit on the head in cricket practice. She's hurt.'

'Where is she?'

'We didn't move her. She's on the pitch.'

'I'm coming right away.' Troy turned to Jonathan, her eyes blazing. 'Look what you've done,' she almost spat at him. 'Making me late. I should have been here.'

She ran to the field, stumbling in her haste, her heart pounding. The girl was on the grass, sprawled out, a bunch of curious spectators peering over her inert body.

'Move back, please, everyone. Let's have some air, some space. Two of you go back to the medical centre and get the stretcher. It's behind the door. Here are my keys. Be quick.' She went down on her knees to the girl. 'Ellen? Ellen? It's Sister Kingsbury. Can you speak? Can you move your fingers? Try to clasp my hand.'

Ellen was pale and drowsy, but not unconscious. A small swelling was appearing on her forehead. Her eyelids were fluttering. Troy was glad to feel a response as Ellen's hand moved in hers.

'That's a good girl,' said Troy. 'You're going to be all right. We'll get you to hospital. Someone tell me what happened again.'

'She was fielding. She went to catch a ball and missed. It hit her on the head. She fell down.' A dozen voices spoke at once.

'She needs a CAT scan,' said Jonathan, on his knees beside Troy, his alert eyes taking in all the body signs.

'I do know that,' Troy said coldly. 'Kindly allow me

to do what is necessary here and now. You're the idiot who made me late.'

'You couldn't have prevented the accident happening even if you had been here,' he said evenly. 'Don't blame yourself. There's no need to carry any guilt.'

'What do you know about it?'

'Believe me, I know about it. I'm carrying guilt all the time,' he said in a low voice. 'My patient in the helicopter died on me.'

Troy was not listening properly. Ellen was being lifted carefully on to the stretcher. Her pulse was erratic and Troy was desperately worried. A computerised axial tomography was the only answer. It was a painless procedure, but would help in the diagnosis of any damage to the skull. Ellen would not feel a thing. Troy would have to phone around to find which hospital could do a scan. A small hospital would not have the equipment.

'Shall I phone around?' Jonathan asked. 'We've got to find a hospital with the right equipment.'

'I know what I'm doing. Don't interfere.'

'I'm only trying to help.'

'You may be able to pull rank on me, but I'm in charge at Belling Hills. If I want your help, I'll ask for it. OK, careful, now. Let's get Ellen back to the medical centre.'

'Don't be a fool,' said Jonathan, refusing to be turned away. His presence was diminishing all others. He was refusing to let his identity be surrendered. He was the surgeon, even if temporarily retired. It was a battle of wills. It seemed to Troy that she was fighting for her very existence as a woman and professional nurse. Yet, even at this moment of extreme emergency, she was fleetingly remembering his kiss and wondering how it would feel if his mouth were to range uninhibitedly over her skin.

'I'll drive her to Plymouth.'

'No need, Troy. I've already phoned for an ambulance. It's on its way.'

She stared at him in numbed shock. How dared he? Yet he was right. Ellen should be in the care of trained paramedics, and she was in no fit state even to park a car. Troy sat back on her heels, the girl's hand limply in hers. She knew when she was beaten. Jonathan had taken the right course. She closed her eyes in misery. She wanted nothing more than to retreat to some safe haven, her cottage, the garden. Yet these comforts were denied her.

'I'm not wasting any more time talking to you. There's a lot to do. Grace must phone Ellen's parents. They'll want to be here.'

'I'm sure Grace has already done that. Will you calm down and stop fussing?'

'I am not fussing,' she fumed, her eyes flashing green sparks. 'And I am perfectly calm. You simply don't understand the responsibilities in a school. It's different to being in a hospital.'

'You have done everything necessary and I predict that Ellen will be out of hospital by the end of the week.'

Jonathan and Joe carried the stretcher back to the medical centre and lifted Ellen gently on to the examination couch. She was drifting in and out of consciousness. Troy prepared a pain-killer and quickly injected it into her arm.

'You're looking at me as if I've done something criminal,' he said, with coolly assessing eyes. 'It was only a cup of coffee.'

'Ellen will probably need an operation.'

'Maybe.' He moved away so that Ellen could not hear the conversation. Patients often overheard snippets that worried them. 'First an X-ray and CAT scan and then a surgeon will use surgical pliers to grasp the bone fragments and lift them back into line with the skull profile. It's a standard procedure for blows to the head like this, a depressed fracture. Your ten-minute coffee has, of course, jeopardised the whole operation, Troy.'

'Don't trivialise what happened. I was late and that was unforgivable. Speed is essential since most of the risk comes from bleeding and possible infection. If anything happens to Ellen. . .'

'You could not have prevented the accident. Are you personally in charge of cricket balls going astray? Anyway, there's the whole subject of cricket being played in a girls' school. It's a bit unusual, isn't it? The decision to include cricket in the curriculum is Grace's. A touch of equality. Anyway, it had only just happened and you went to Ellen as fast as possible.'

'Not exactly true. The girls were waiting in the courtyard.'

'Minutes, then. You're talking about a few minutes.'

'Minutes can be vital.'

'The girl is not comatose and she's not vomiting, both the classic symptoms that the dura membrane has been penetrated.' Jonathan heaved an irritated sigh. 'If you are determined to feel guilty, then nothing I can say will change your mind. You did everything possible, as fast as possible, and when you've cooled down you might have the good sense to acknowledge that fact.'

A neuro-surgeon operated on Ellen late that night. Only a tiny patch of hair was shaved off. Afterwards she was moved to Intensive Care with half-hourly checks of blood-pressure, temperature and pupil response and movement. She responded so well that the checks graduated to four-hourly.

Her parents flew down from Scotland and were soon at the bedside of their pale-faced daughter, who was now wearing a lop-sided head bandage and a sheepish grin.

Her fellow pupils were curious about Ellen's injury and Troy explained the procedure in simple terms. She believed in taking the mystique out of operations, sure that it helped to disperse excessive fear. She always said that the prick of an injection might hurt for a second, rather than saying, 'This isn't going to hurt.'

'But will her brain be damaged?' her best friend asked anxiously.

'Not at all,' said Troy. 'The skull is like a helmet protecting the brain. If the helmet has a dent in it, then it makes sense to straighten it out. Ellen will feel a bit sore this morning, but not too much. I'm sure she'll bounce back. Only not too much bouncing around for a while. She'll need some peace and quiet for a few days, then she may go home with her parents for a short time.'

Troy knew she would have two patients to keep an eye on. The girl who had thrown the cricket ball was also upset. She was worried about Ellen suffering lasting damage and was depressed about the whole matter. She needed the reassurance of seeing Ellen take up normal school activities to prevent any deep emotional scars.

'When Ellen returns to school she'll need a couple of minders,' said Troy. 'To stop people asking too many questions or bumping into her. Perhaps you two would like to do that?' She smiled at Ellen's best friend and the girl who had thrown the ball. 'Good. That's settled, then. You'll probably have to stop Ellen rushing straight back on to the cricket pitch too.'

The following days were saturated in sunshine; the earth heated up and the pupils changed into short-sleeved summer uniform. The Devon hills reflected back the sunshine, the dappled grass fresh and sweet-smelling, life breathing through the russet earth. Sheep dotted the hills like slow-moving mushrooms, and clusters of caravans appeared at weekends as the tourist industry got into stride.

Jonathan waited outside the medical centre in the noon heat, pacing restlessly, his hair tousled by the light wind. Troy was returning from taking a health class, longing to change into something cooler. But her heart leaped when she saw Jonathan, much to her disgust. What was it about the man? Her throat constricted, making it difficult to speak.

'Y-yes?'

She had been deliberately keeping away from the cottage, despite the warmth of the balmy evenings that beckoned her to the garden. She missed the tranquillity of the whitebeam and the privacy of the tiny garden perched above the cliffs. She had taken a book and some apples into a shady part of the school grounds, but immediately became an object of interest, and was aware of small girls viewing her eccentricity from a distance.

'How is our cricket enthusiast?' he asked. He seemed apprehensive, yet she knew he had the ability to switch from boyish charm to steely authoritarianism.

'Not quite so enthusiastic, but doing well. She'll be back before half-term. Can I help you? Is another physio due?'

'You know how I hate asking these favours,' he said drily. 'It makes me feel helpless.'

'You could hire a taxi,' she pointed out.

'Not so pleasant as your company and being driven in my own car,' he returned. 'Besides, the tourist season is hotting up. Have you tried getting a taxi recently? I've also noticed that you rarely take any time off. I thought perhaps we could have lunch in Dartmouth. Grace says it's a very pretty place with lots of old houses and steep streets as well as all the river boats churning up and down.'

'Don't you ever get the message?' said Troy, exasperated. 'I'm not into the social scene. Look what happened last time. I was late back and a girl was hurt.'

'But this time you would not be late back. It would be your day off,' Jonathan said patiently. 'I presume you are covered by Nurse Norwood on your day off.'

'Am I hearing you correctly? You want me to spend my precious day off ferrying you to the hospital, then hanging about for the dubious pleasure of a meal with you?' Troy was lost in amazement, but not admiration of his impudence.

'No, Troy, there's really much more,' he said with a hesitant smile that accelerated her heartbeats. 'I want to talk to you. I think we ought to try and get things straightened out between us. You wouldn't enjoy my home cooking, so I'd like to take you out.'

'Have we got something to talk about?'

'Yes, I think we have. We got off to a bad start and we ought to get to know each other properly. After all, we have a lot in common.'

'Yes, my cottage,' Troy could not resist saying.

'Like guilt. We could talk about guilt. I could tell you a story about guilt that would make your hair curl.'

There was a profound stillness about him as Jonathan spoke those words, as if they cost him a great deal. He dominated the scene even in that small, sun-dappled stone courtyard. Wall-brown butterflies darted among the potted geraniums, the eyes on each wing ready to alarm any predators. The heat hummed off the baking stones. Troy did not question her own feelings as she changed her mind. She sensed his need to talk and gave in to her curiosity.

'All right,' she said. 'Tomorrow, then. I'll make an appointment for you.'

'I've already got one,' he said. 'Eleven-thirty.'

Troy regretted her acceptance. She almost threw it back at him. He had been so sure of her that he'd already made an appointment. He was so infuriatingly superior all the time. Yet perhaps they'd made it for him on his last visit. . .

He made no move to go, his eyes searching hers. 'One more favour. Could you give me a quick lesson on how to work your computer? You half said you would. I can't make head nor tail of mine. Textscreen, start-of-day disc, disckit. . .the handbook is written in a foreign language, I swear.'

Troy knew what he meant. At the beginning she had been on the point of sending the medical centre's computer back. 'But I half said I wouldn't,' she reminded him. 'They invented computer jargon for the sole purpose of confusing people like you and me.'

'You said I'm supposed to be using these. . .' He wriggled his fingers stiffly. 'To keep them moving.'

Troy took his hand in hers and flexed the fingers. They were long and brown, with clean, well cut nails. Nice-looking for a man's hand, not too large. A surgeon did not want large hands. His skin was warm, smooth and dry. Peter's hands had always been moist.

'They are improving,' she said, concern in her voice. She tried not to let the tingle in her own fingers travel too far or to look beyond the fine dark hairs on his wrist. 'You should do the exercises regularly.'

'Perhaps you would show me, Sister,' he said, the blue in his eyes deepening with amusement. 'Most surgeons are absolutely useless when it comes to their own health. We make lousy patients.'

'That's true. Pigheaded, obstinate, opinionated.'

'You have a charming way of putting it, Sister. Tomorrow, then? It's a date?'

'Tomorrow. And you can come in now and have

your first word-processing lesson. I must be mad. I've got more than enough to do.'

But their tomorrow never came. Troy was woken by the telephone in the early hours of the morning. It was Grace, her voice anxious.

'Care staff have discovered two empty beds, one in Third and one in Fourth. The girls were both there at lights out, a little subdued, but nothing out of the ordinary.'

'Who's missing?' Troy slid out of bed and started pulling on some clothes.

'Gillian Pritchard and Lucy Warren.'

'Lucy Warren. . .but she's such a quiet youngster. I wouldn't have thought she'd have the courage to run away, especially at night.'

'I think Gillian is the ringleader. She's always in trouble. She had a detention today for not handing in work.'

'Are you informing the police?'

'Not yet. I know I should, but I'd like to get the girls back without any publicity. It would put Belling Hills in a bad light. We think they've gone towards the moors.'

'What makes you think that?' Troy knew what was coming, tucking the receiver under her chin and tying the laces of her walking-boots.

'Apparently they were talking about it. Some girls in the dining-room overheard them at supper. Hound Tor, Bull Gate and Maiden's Sorrow were mentioned. I suppose they intend to hide out on the moors. It might take days to find them.'

'It would. It's very wild and wind-swept on the moors. Maiden's Sorrow is a desolate spot.'

'You're an experienced walker, aren't you, Troy? And you know the moors well. Could you. . .?'

'I could go ahead and try to cut them off. I know the ground better than they do. They won't be going very fast, even if they have a head start and have managed to hitch a lift to Dartmoor.'

'They took their bikes. They're both missing from the bicycle shed.'

'Heaven help them.'

'Take Jonathan's car.'

'Nothing but the best,' said Troy, fastening an anorak. 'I'll keep in touch, let you know what's happening. I'll borrow Jonathan's portable telephone.'

'What a blessing that Jonathan is here,' said Grace, revealing the strain in her voice. It was a headmistress's nightmare. 'At times like these, one needs a man around.'

'Yes, he's such a comfort,' said Troy, glad that Grace could not see her expression. She was going to enjoy waking him up at two in the morning to borrow his phone.

But Jonathan was already up, dressed in walking-clothes, cords and jersey, and a waterproof anorak. He was making a Thermos of coffee in the kitchen.

'Grace phoned. I'm coming with you. Two pairs of eyes,' he added as he saw Troy starting to protest. She gave in without a word, beyond thinking, beyond caring. He was right, dammit, as always.

'Phone, map, compass, flashlamp,' she checked. She could barely trust herself to speak. His uncomfortably candid eyes were reading right through her. 'Let's get going.'

The E-Type handled like a dream, its lights piercing the dark with strong, sweeping beams. Troy drove with confidence. The roads were empty and she knew the way to the southern edge of Dartmoor. She had walked the moors so many times that first summer in Devon, letting the landscape heal the raw wounds.

'Hound Tor is open moorland,' she said in the warm, intimate darkness of the car. 'It's rough moorland, pretty steep, simply beautiful views in daylight. I've walked it many times. You'll remember Lucy Warren. . .she's the red-haired girl we found playing truant on the dunes. She's one of the runaways. There's something odd about that girl, but I don't know what.'

'Have you checked with her teachers?'

'Apparently she lacks concentration, but that's nothing new. Also she tends to hang back, not to join in things, particularly sports. But apart from these vague observations, and her long list of minor upsets, there's nothing really wrong with her.'

'And the other girl?'

'Gillian is a real madcap, always in trouble, does as little work as possible, a ringleader in any escapade. She was caught organising a gambling-den in the science lab after hours last year. They were racing guinea-pigs. She was taking the bets.'

'The girl will make a fortune one day.'

The moors loomed darkly on the horizon, etched against a grey sky already touched with a lightening dawn. Outcrops of black rock stood like fingers of doom, pointing skywards, ageless and wrapped in legend.

Troy parked as close as possible to the bridle track which began the uphill climb. They crossed a stream on stepping-stones, climbed a stone-posted gap, then strode up a narrow, grassy, gated lane. Jonathan was carrying their supplies in a rucksack, leaving her hands free to use the flashlamp.

As she climbed a stile, he swung her down and held her boldly against him. For a moment she was cradled against his chest, fitting in all the right places, and all her feelings swept back, her whole being ignited with longing.

'Isn't this better than arguing?' he said, his hand deep in her soft hair. 'This is how I imagine friends. . . lovers might be.'

'It's just make-believe, a dream.' Troy trembled. 'It's not real life.'

'Real life could be better if we were friends instead of behaving as if we hated the sight of each other.'

'If this is behaving as if we hated each other,' said Troy, catching the hand that was tangled in her hair, 'then I'd say it would be pretty dangerous if we became good friends.'

'We'd make a good team,' he went on, resting his chin on the top of her head. 'The first-aid classes are useful, but there is a limit to my bandaging skills, and the girls get the giggles every time I demonstrate mouth-to-mouth resuscitation on the model. Why not let me do some night duty? I'm used to working nights. It would give your loyal assistant some time at home.'

'She gets all the holidays off,' said Troy. 'It's part of

the arrangement. Often she doesn't come in if there are no patients in the sick-bay.'

'I could assist at morning surgery. Sometimes there's a queue a mile long.'

'What an exaggeration. I hope your surgical perception of lengths is more accurate. All right, if that's what you want, you can do morning surgery on my day off. But I'm afraid I won't be able to wait around to take you to your physio. I'll be long gone.'

She felt his hold tighten. 'What a little tyrant you are. You'd terrorise my theatre staff.'

Troy strained away from him. No man should be aware of the effect he had. 'Now will you please let me go?' she said lightly. 'This is not allowed.'

'I seldom do as I am told,' he said.

CHAPTER FIVE

THE lonely moorland was a bleak setting for Troy's chaotic thoughts and wordless panic as Jonathan held her. She tried to wriggle out of his hold.

'This isn't helping to find the girls,' she said.

He dropped his arms immediately and let her go. He had been caught off guard and now he was annoyed with himself. Damn the moors and their dawn magic. A hundred times he had vowed to keep his distance, but every time he saw Troy all his good intentions vanished with one look into her deep green eyes.

'Merely assisting you over a stile.'

'I can manage on my own.'

'I'll remember that if we meet a herd of horned moorland cattle.'

Low rocky mounds and a solitary megalithic standing stone reminded Troy of the prehistoric peoples who had lived and died on these wild hills, the last wilderness in England. No one really knew why the standing stones were there, nor the even stranger stone rows casting their complex line shadows as the sky lightened.

'Look, over there, stone rows. . .' said Jonathan with a degree of interest in his voice. He had never seen them before. 'I wonder why they built them.'

'Runways?' she suggested. 'For space ships?'

She could hardly imagine the human activity of those people of four and five thousand years back. The only reality was this tall, powerful man striding alongside her, occasionally stopping to scan the open, rolling heather-clad granite uplands as the first tinges of dawn streaked the sky. The moor broadened out to a grassy terrace and they paused to catch their breath.

'What are we supposed to do?' asked Jonathan. 'Call out their names? Hi, Gillian? Lucy?'

'I think that would scare them off. They will be exhausted and cold, and probably sheltering somewhere, trying to keep warm and sleep. I'm really worried, Jonathan. Even experienced walkers can get caught out on these moors. There are these soggy wet clefts between the rocks called feather beds, all too easy to fall into. And you can't see them. The sphagnum moss tops them like a blanket.'

Dark brown shapes moved across the horizon, cropping, manes tossing. 'Look. . .ponies,' said Troy with a wide, radiant smile. She loved the fearless little creatures. 'They're harmless, but the shaggy black moorland cattle can look frightening.'

'The girls will probably think they've met the Hounds of the Baskervilles.'

'That's exactly what I'm worried about. Girls of that age can be over-imaginative. This area has three high points—Hound Tor, Bull Gate and Maiden's Sorrow. Let's comb it, looking everywhere that might provide some shelter.'

'Don't go too far ahead of me,' said Jonathan, as Troy began to climb higher. 'We might meet one of those doggone Hounds.'

'Just freeze it one of your icy glares.'

The dawn was beginning to lighten the sky with

white fingers, painting from a palette of pastels; first the palest of pink washes spilled from a watery brush, eclipsing the murkiness of the night. It was fragile and beautiful. Troy longed to stand and watch the changing colours.

Jonathan was thinking the same, but wishing that he and Troy were walking together as friends, not on this errand of haystack searching. That smile when she had caught sight of the ponies. . .would she ever smile like that at him? He sensed the unhappiness she hid so well and cursed himself for adding to it with clumsy overtures and the ill-conceived remarks.

He could see how the rocks got their names. The wind and erosion had carved them into weird and wonderful shapes, exposed still more as the ground around them was worn away.

'Some of these cairns are burial grounds,' said Troy. 'Not my idea of an ideal campsite.' Her head was swimming from the stiff climb. The stony track was running with water and she stepped from side to side, zigzagging upwards, trying to find a drier route.

'Are we ascending a riverbed?' Jonathan grumbled.

'Looks like it. These springs suddenly appear, then disappear. It's drier over here.' She leaped from stone to stone, as lightly as a pony herself, but then her foot slipped on a patch of wet moss and she came crashing down.

'Ouch,' she cried as her shoulder took the weight of the fall, catching on a sharp edge. She lay, winded.

Jonathan was at her side in seconds, visions of broken ankles and splints and helicopters to be summoned racing into his mind. A blinding flash seared his eyes as he relived that other crash, burning debris flying through his memory.

'Troy, are you all right?' His long, skilful fingers touched her legs and ankles carefully, felt along the slender bones. She tried to brush him aside.

'Go away, I'm perfectly all right,' she said, struggling to sit up, her hands sliding on the slippery rock.

He put his arms under her armpits and hauled her to her feet. 'Are you sure?' The unexpected tenderness was more than she could bear. She twisted her head away, not wanting to see the concern in those piercing eyes, his sardonic features softened.

'Of course,' she said, annoyed with herself. 'I only slipped on a wet patch.'

'Try standing.'

'I am standing.'

Her exasperated reply broke the tension and they both laughed. The sound carried on the wind, seeming to echo on the rocks. He took her hands. 'I'm glad,' he said.

She wondered if he was going to kiss her again, but this time he was wary. She put a halt to her wayward thoughts, aware of her disappointment, mixed with annoyance at her weakness.

'Ah, I spy two bicycles,' she said.

The two bicycles lay abandoned against a rock, covered in mud and grass, spokes twisted, one chain hanging off.

'They can't be far off now,' said Troy. 'It must have taken a superhuman effort to drag their bikes up here. Well, despite what I feel about litter on the moors, they'll have to stay until someone can retrieve them. That next outcrop is Maiden's Sorrow.'

The group of rocks ahead did have the vague shape of a young woman, bent, her head resting on a flat-faced rock like a table. It had once been a taller edifice, but time had tumbled rocks around her feet like discarded playthings.

'I can see how it came by its name,' said Jonathan.

'That rock has been there for thousands of centuries,' said Troy, seeing the shape of the still maiden so clearly that she became real. 'There's a legend about the rock, about telling the maiden your troubles. Time softens the edges of pain.'

'Does it?'

'I think so. It's the way we are made, to carry on living despite what happens.'

'Are your sorrows softening? Is time helping you?'

'Yes, in a way. I feel much calmer now. It's a wonder Grace gave me the post. The strain must have shown on my face.'

'Perhaps that's why she gave you the job.'

'Your hands will recover in time. You know that,' said Troy. 'You must have said the same a hundred times to patients with similar injuries. They were expected to believe you. Now you've got to believe yourself.'

'It's not so easy when you are both patient and doctor. You know all the chances, the gamble; nothing is black and white.'

They heard a whimper and stopped and listened, straining their ears. The wind was sighing through the grasses, filling their ears with a constant moan and rustle.

'Over there?' Troy thought she caught a glimpse of a splash of light reddish hair. She hurried towards the bright anoraked shapes huddled down by some rocks trying to find some shelter.

'Babes in the grass, I presume,' she said.

The girls did not deserve breakfast in a local hostelry, but that was what they got. Jonathan insisted. They were both cold, wet and starving, and he said it was sensible to warm them up and feed them before the drive back to Belling Hills. Troy phoned Grace to put her mind at rest.

'Your brother is treating them to a slap-up breakfast,' she said darkly. 'I've just left them tucking into scrambled eggs on toast, orange juice and coffee.'

'Coffee?' Grace sounded shocked. 'They are not allowed coffee.'

'They are also not allowed to eat out when they have run away from school and we've been searching half of Dartmoor in the pitch-dark for hours looking for them,' Troy pointed out. 'I hope you will tell your brother that we are running a boarding-school, not a high-class hotel for delinquents. He'll probably take them shopping next to buy dry clothes.'

'I'm relieved that they are both safe, of course. But I'll be phoning their parents to come and see me straight away. Don't worry, Troy, they will both be confined to school for the rest of the term.'

'I'm glad to hear that. I thought perhaps you might be going to throw them a welcome-home party.'

'Sarcasm does not suit you, Sister Kingsbury,' said Grace. 'But I do understand your dismay. My brother is too kind-hearted.'

Troy could not bring herself to answer. Kind-hearted was not an overall term she would have applied to Jonathan Howard. She could think of a whole string of stronger words.

The girls were quiet on the drive back, tucked up into the back of Jonathan's car, wearing the spare sweaters Troy had thought to bring along. It appeared that Gillian was the prime mover in the plan to run away.

'It's my parents,' she had said, choking back her tears. 'They keep on and on at me about these exams. I hate exams. I can't do them. I won't do them. I don't want to take them.'

'We'll talk about this when we get back to Belling Hills,' said Troy. 'This is obviously something we all need to talk about.'

Troy knew about parental pressure. She had seen it before. It might account for Gillian's continual bad behaviour and flouting of the rules.

'Shall I be sent down? Expelled?'

'I don't know,' said Troy wearily. She suddenly realised that she had missed the dawn. It had all happened when they had found the girls, given them hot drinks, then hurried the frightened, shivering pair down the moors to civilisation. 'You'll have to wait and see. It'll be Miss Howard's decision.'

Troy was dead tired and wanted to sleep and sleep. Her shoulder was aching. Thank goodness she didn't have to take morning surgery. It was supposed to be her day off, but she knew she wanted to see both sets of parents. Lucy puzzled her. She did not seem to have a reason for running away and didn't answer any of Troy's questions. She said she'd gone along because Gillian had asked her to. It didn't make sense.

It seemed to take hours to get the girls bathed, then in bed in the sick-bay with Karen Norwood on duty. There was no need to call in Dr Wright. There was nothing physically wrong with them that a good sleep wouldn't cure. The sun had risen and it was a glorious day. Troy drove Jonathan back to the cottage, practically asleep at the wheel, stopping outside with a crunch of brakes.

'Come on, sleepyhead,' he said, helping her out of the driving-seat. 'Up half the night. It's time you went to bed.'

'Ouch,' she murmured, leaning against him, intensely aware of his closeness, suddenly nervous.

'What's the matter?' he asked, pushing open the door and propelling her indoors.

'My shoulder. It hurts.'

'You definitely need to see a doctor.'

'I am seeing a doctor.' She opened her eyes. Dear heavens, he was taking her upstairs to her own bed. She could not believe it. Her own bed. . .

'Is this a guided tour? I know this used to be my bedroom,' she said. 'I don't want to see what you've done to it.'

'Don't worry,' he soothed. 'Nothing has changed. Just a few books.'

'A few books?' Her glance took in the piles of heavy medical tomes. 'Half a library.' She also noticed the navy silk dressing-gown behind the door, the comfortable suede slippers on the floor and a sleek radio alarm by the bed.

He was carrying her across the room to the bed, her bed. She had to twine her arms around his neck to stop herself from falling. It was such a pleasurable experience, to feel him close to her and to smell the heady musk of his skin. Yet she was so tired that he could not possibly have any intention but to let her sleep.

Feelings that she had long forgotten and thought lost stirred in her body, making her limbs tremble. She remembered nights of lovemaking many years ago that she had thought perfect, but now she was not so sure about them. She longed to be loved again, to feel passionate kisses and caresses, to give her body to a man that she loved.

She steadied her hand on Jonathan's sleeve as he lowered her on to the bed. It was a torment to have him so near, to want him to stay, yet have to make him leave. But did she have to? Her heart was thudding violently as she felt herself being drawn towards him. It was not only a physical desire but a deeply emotional one; Troy wanted to allow herself to love him, to be part of his life, to become someone special to him.

It had been a long time since anyone had cared for her, cared what happened to her. If ever. She had never been sure about her husband's feelings. She was frightened of what was happening to her body, the way it was responding to Jonathan's closeness. He touched her serene face with slow, gentle strokes, his mouth breathing a sweetness on her parted lips.

'Troy, darling...?'

In the silence, Jonathan moved about, opening a window, drawing the curtains against splintered fragments of brilliance. He was letting her decide, and Troy was unable to make such a decision. She wanted him so much. She wanted to be a woman again in a man's arms. She was tired of being the proper and oh, so correct Sister Kingsbury; she wanted to be a seductive Helen of Troy, driving a man mad with her body.

She had fallen deeply in love with this dark and awkward man. It was unbelievable. He was so totally wrong for her, and yet every sense within her was saying that he might be totally right.

Jonathan was breathing heavily and, as he put her against the pillows, his hand slipped round her waist, under her rising breasts. The brush of his hand was electrifying. She tried to draw away from the touch, but there was nowhere to go.

'Your shoulder. . .?' he said huskily.

'It doesn't hurt now,' she said in a low voice, surprised that it did not. Its dull ache was nothing. She had forgotten all about her shoulder in the dim intimacy of these enclosed walls. 'I can't think why. . .'

She could hardly see the whitebeam against the window, her friendly tapping tree. The bulk of Jonathan was blocking her view. Her eyes were heavy with sleep in the milky, silky stillness of the room.

'Troy. . .are you sure? Is this what you want?'

She nodded, her expression transparent, her fingers curling through his hair, loving the feel of its thick texture, finding the inward curve of his muscled neck, pulling him down to her, loving the look in his glittering eyes.

He was tasting her lips with a soft, insistent pressure of kisses that were barely a breath apart—not at all like that other hard and arrogant kiss that had made her wild with anger. She felt herself melting in his arms, willing him to touch her, wanting him to go further.

He reached down to take off her boots. He made quick work of her belt and zip, pulling off the muddy jeans with the ease and precision of a casualty officer. She held up her arms and he eased the shirt over her head, not wanting to fumble with buttons. He moved away and she heard the thump of his own boots falling on the floor, and later the sound of clothes being taken off.

Moments later she felt Jonathan slide in beside her and the soft hair of his naked chest press against her. He flung an arm across her waist and she leaned against him, weariness coming in waves.

'Go to sleep,' he murmured. 'It'll be good for you. . .'

'Jonathan, please. . .don't you want me?'

'Doesn't this tell you?' he murmured. His mouth opened hers and he drowned himself in the sweetness of her taste. Her lips were as soft as velvet, and the longing of the lonely years overflowed into the way he touched her silky skin. He cupped her breast, tentatively, afraid she might push him away, but she didn't, and his fingers found a rosy nipple which tensed almost immediately into a tiny peak.

Troy caught her breath. The touch was exquisite.

She had forgotten what it was like to be moulded by a man's hand. And this was Jonathan, his face dark in the gloom of the room, the muscles of his shoulders bunched as he kept his weight from crushing her. Yet she wanted to be crushed; she wanted to feel his full weight on her. She wanted to be filled with him.

She stroked his long back, the muscled arms, the strong neck, her hands delving into the wiry hair on his chest. His body was good and clean and strong and she loved every inch of it. This was why she had waited, been so cautious. It was a first time all over again, wiping out bad memories, her feelings blossoming like a hungry flower.

He was being so gentle, as if he was scared. Maybe it was a long time for him too. Perhaps his relationships in London had never developed. Perhaps he had never allowed them to.

The joy of this thought sent her desire surging, and she pulled him towards her, her lips telling his mouth how much she wanted him. She twisted her legs round him, rubbing his hardened calves with her heels. A long shudder went through him.

'This is madness,' he said. 'You should sleep.'

'No. . .' But she was fighting waves of weariness.

'Doctor's orders,' he groaned. He buried his face in the fragrance of her lace-veiled breasts and she could feel him shaking. Their hesitance was paining him too, and she took comfort from that knowledge.

'When we wake up?' she asked hopefully, feeling her senses slipping away. She never heard his answer. She slept for several hours with Jonathan's arms wrapped around her.

When she eventually awoke to find the afternoon sun streaming into the room, Jonathan had gone. For a moment she felt utterly bereft, as if he had died or scorned her. Then good sense took over and she was glad he had gone. It gave her a chance to regain her composure. Her face burned as she remembered how much she had wanted Jonathan, and the abandon of her kisses.

Troy remembered that the parents of the runaway girls would be arriving that afternoon, and she ought to speak to them. Grace would be busy explaining the seriousness of the girls' actions and the withdrawal of privileges. Troy wanted to find out the motive for the girls' desperate escapade.

She swung her legs over the side of the bed and stretched her arms. She felt so good. Now she knew that there might be some future for her. . . Her body could still respond to a man, if it was the right man.

She threw on her clothes and hurried out of the cottage, for once without bitterness. Jonathan was not around. She went back to her flat, showered, and washed the dust out of her long hair. She decided not to wear her formal sister's uniform; her interview with the parents might go better if she looked more informal in a slim linen skirt and cream shirt.

Lucy Warren's parents were waiting in the main entrance hall of the school. They were a well dressed middle-aged couple who looked worried and distraught, as if Lucy's behaviour was quite beyond them. Troy introduced herself and they seemed pleased to sit down on the tapestry sofas in the pleasant waiting-hall and talk to her.

'Lucy is such a nice girl,' said Troy. 'None of us can understand why she would do such a silly thing. We've never had any trouble from her before.'

'She's always a good girl,' said Mrs Warren, wringing her gloves. 'She does what she's told at home.'

'Is she as quiet at home?' Troy asked casually.

'Quiet?'

The parents exchanged bewildered glances. 'Quiet?' said Mr Warren. 'I suppose she is a bit quiet. We have a business to run, a wholesale clothing business, so we're both out at work all day. We don't see much of Lucy in the holidays, just some evenings and weekends.'

'So who looks after Lucy?'

'We have a couple,' said Mrs Warren with some enthusiasm. 'They've been with us for years. They look after Lucy as if she were their own child. We trust them implicitly.'

'You're very lucky,' said Troy. 'By the way, did you know that Lucy has made some excuse for not attending most of the games sessions this summer — swimming, rounders, cricket?'

'That's very odd,' said her father. 'We thought she enjoyed swimming. She used to.'

Troy did not mention Lucy's lack of concentration in lessons, nor her frequent headaches and stomach upsets. The girl had become a regular attender at the medical centre. Troy almost dreaded seeing the girl's wan face in the waiting-room. And that watchfulness, which was so disconcerting.

'Perhaps it would help if you or your wife could

spend more time with her during the holidays,' said Troy, wondering if that was part of the trouble.

Mrs Warren looked flustered. 'Well, I suppose I could take some time off. We are so busy. . .'

'Why not take Lucy along with you on some days? All young girls are interested in clothes. There might be some aspect of your business which would hold her attention for a few hours. Then she could have lunch with you, even if it's only a working sandwich; get her to make the coffee. . .'

Troy broke off, slightly embarrassed. She realised she had no idea what the Warrens' clothing business might be. It could be expensive designer clothes or cheap, down-market ready-mades.

The door to the headmistress's study opened and Grace's secretary came out. 'Mr and Mrs Warren? Miss Howard will see you now.'

'Shall we be able to see Lucy?' Mrs Warren asked, rising.

'Of course. I'll find her.'

'Thank you for your kindness, Sister,' said Mr Warren. 'It's much appreciated.'

Troy smiled at the couple. They seemed genuinely concerned, even if too occupied with work to give their only child much time.

Gillian's parents were coming out of Grace's study, both looking somewhat flushed and annoyed. Grace had obviously made it clear that Gillian had been the ringleader in this escapade and that the night on the moors had been both foolish and dangerous for both girls.

Troy went to greet them. 'Mr and Mrs Pritchard, I'm

Sister Kingsbury. I wonder if I could have a word with you?'

They were a much younger couple, svelte, slim and tanned, the trappings of wealth and success evident in their clothes, watches, bags, shoes and fashionable haircuts. Troy's courage sank. Perhaps she should have worn her uniform. They would probably demolish her with a few brittle, cutting words. But she thought of the troubled expression in Gillian's eyes and knew she had to help the girl.

'We want to see our daughter.'

'Naturally. But just a few moments of your time. . .'

Gillian's mother lounged on the sofa and crossed her long legs, swinging a narrow lizardskin shoe. 'We haven't got much time. We're catching a plane back to Zurich tonight.'

'I think it's important that we should talk about the entrance exams that Gillian is due to take this term. She seems to be very worried about them.'

'And so she should be,' said Mr Pritchard, taking a thin cigar from a silver case and lighting up. 'It's important that she passes. We've set out hearts on her moving on to Ruddick College as soon as she's old enough.'

'I went to Ruddick,' said Mrs Pritchard, looking at her perfect nails.

Troy swallowed a retort heavy with sarcasm. It would not help Gillian if she antagonised the parents.

'Gillian's talents might lie in another direction. She might not be so academic. We can't all be clever.'

'The girl is clever enough. She just needs to apply herself. It's only a matter of passing a few exams.'

'Has it occurred to you that this pressure may be too much for her? Perhaps she doesn't want to go to Ruddick.'

'Of course she wants to go to Ruddick,' said her mother complacently. 'Most girls would give their eye-teeth.'

Troy could see that the parents were not in a mood to listen, both restless and anxious to be on their plane to Zurich. They were both set on their daughter passing these exams and probably told her so in every letter and phone call. No wonder she had run away.

Troy stood up, very tall and correct, every inch a matriarchal sister. She could do it even without wearing a uniform. It was a knack.

'It's nice to have met you, Mr and Mrs Pritchard. We are able to understand our pupils even more after meeting their parents. When you see Gillian now, it would be tactless to mention these exams. I suggest you make your visit a pleasant one.'

Without waiting for a reply, Troy nodded and left the hall. It was still technically her day off, after all. She intended to rescue what was left of it with a swim in the pool. It would be empty now. The girls would soon be going into supper.

She loved going into a still pool, watching her first strokes ripple across the smooth glassy blue surface. Then she dived under the water with long, slow pulls of her arms, pretending she was a dolphin, turning and twisting, coming up for air, face streaming.

The last rays of the sun were rosy on the glass walls of the pool, throwing long shadows across the tiled floor. Troy suddenly realised that she was not alone.

Someone else had arrived, the door banging. She dived under again, not wanting her solitude to be spoilt, not wanting to share the pool.

She saw lean brown legs flash past her in the water, arms ploughing a fast crawl, and, with a jolt, her heart knew, even if she did not immediately recognise the wet figure. She came up, struggling for air.

'Trying to break underwater records, Sister?' Jonathan asked, breaking the surface at her side.

She smiled hesistantly at him, water sticking to her eyes. So much depended on how he treated her now. If he was cool, her heart would break and she would know that she had thrown herself at him for nothing.

The water slapped against the silk of her thighs as she waited for him to speak, her gaze never leaving him.

CHAPTER SIX

THE pause seemed endless. Troy tried to marshal her thoughts into some coherency. She was overjoyed to see him and yet worried that this first meeting after sleeping in each other's arms might be difficult. His face did not betray his feelings. He stood firmly in the deep water, the matt of dark hair on his chest glistening.

She averted her eyes, remembering its softness against her skin only too clearly. The jade water washed around her, cooling her burning flesh.

'We didn't break any records in bed, did we?' she said, her normal directness going straight to what was worrying her. 'You weren't there when I woke up. It was awful. You had gone.'

A muscle tightened in his jaw. 'I couldn't sleep. I was restless, so I got up in case I disturbed you. It was obvious that you needed your sleep.'

'I also needed you to be with me,' said Troy, with the same transparent honesty. 'At least I thought I did then.'

'But now you have your doubts? I thought you might have. I didn't want to be someone you would regret in the morning, Troy. I like you too much for that.'

His eyes narrowed as he slowly examined her tensed figure under the water. She wished she had not worn such a revealing swimsuit, but since she normally swam alone the cut-away sides had never mattered. She let herself sink deeper into the water, trying to cover her embarrassment.

He caught her bare shoulders and stopped her sinking further. 'Don't try to hide yourself,' he coaxed. 'You're very lovely. I only want to look at you. It would have been very easy to stay with you and have the pleasure of waking you up, but I think I know the kind of person you are, Troy. There has to be love, doesn't there? You have to love the man in your arms, and one day you'll find someone more suitable — someone who isn't a freak, a cripple. I'm sure you will.'

Jonathan was only being kind, but it sounded so patronising that Troy had trouble keeping rein on her uncertain temper. Her eyes mirrored her bewilderment. This was no time to tell him that she loved him. He obviously felt nothing for her beyond a slight amusement at her impetuous actions.

She shivered in the water, remembering the touch of his fingers and the way her response had rocketed out of control. If this was how she reacted to a few kisses, she did not dare think of any other, more abandoned circumstances. She wondered if she would ever feel at peace again. She could not trust her own body.

'Of course,' she said vaguely. 'It was simply overtiredness and the comfortable, familiar feeling of being so at home in my own bed for once with someone nice.'

She realised instantly that it sounded all wrong. It could be misconstrued. A darkly hostile gleam shot into his eyes. His hands dropped from her shoulders.

'It had not occurred to me before. But of course you

must have entertained friends—male friends—many times at your cottage. How convenient. Well out of sight of the school, off the beaten track, no one to tell tales. The perfect romantic love-nest.'

'That is not what I meant and you know it,' she snapped, in a tone that denied every word. 'Trust you to jump to the wrong conclusion. I have never had anyone to stay in the cottage, nor has anything remotely romantic gone on. Unless you count several wild games of scrabble with Mrs Lawson, the history teacher.'

'You were so upset when I took over the cottage. I did wonder why. Now I know why,' he continued relentlessly. 'And I thought you were homesick. Man-sick might be a more apt description of your unwillingness.'

'Man-sick? I don't understand,' said Troy desperately. 'You're trying to turn round everything I say. There hasn't been anyone in my life since. . .since my husband.'

She stopped abruptly, realising that she had not mentioned Peter before. Jonathan did not know she had been married. No one, except Grace, knew she had been married. She had kept it a closet marriage. 'And there's not likely to be anyone new if I keep meeting men like you,' she added with spirit.

His eyes were suddenly blazing and her throat constricted with fear; she was frightened at the change in him. She had never seen him so angry or with such pain in his eyes.

'Your husband? This is incredible. . .and you didn't feel it necessary to tell me? I'm glad I went instead to my physio. Joe saved me from a fate worse than adultery with his offer of a lift in the school minibus. So you're married, Troy. . . I'm glad I found out in time.'

His laconic voice gave away nothing. But his actions did. He sank back into the water and began a fast, vicious crawl down the length of the pool, a wave of spray hiding his gaunt face.

Troy clambered out of the pool, shaking. She was deeply hurt and upset. It was a grainy evening now that the sun had gone, wisps of clouds feather-boning the sky. She felt too spent to do anything but drag on her sandals and ivory towelling robe and hurry back to the flat as quickly as possible.

She slammed the door behind her and locked it. She had had enough of Dr Jonathan Howard. With a jolt she realised it was nearly twenty-four hours since they had set out to find the girls on the barren heights of Dartmoor. It seemed years ago. Jonathan was dangerous because he was sexy, or was it the other way round? Maybe he was sexually attractive because he was dangerous.

She shuddered in her clammy swimsuit and peeled it away from her skin, rubbing herself dry. She would stay here, in her bat's attic, make some supper, read a decent book and put Jonathan right out of her mind. She needed time to get her feelings straight, to decide how she was going to cope with the rest of the term. He would be gone soon, back to London, and the sooner the better.

It was harder than she thought to concentrate on her

book, her thoughts constantly going back to the pool, and she was not sorry to be interrupted by the telephone.

'Sister Kingsbury.'

'Troy? Oh, I'm so glad you are in. Can you come round to my flat right now?' It was Grace Howard and she sounded agitated. 'It's quite urgent.'

'What's happened? Do I need my medical bag?'

'No, Troy. This isn't going to be a wound you can see to stitch up. It's something far more difficult.'

Sarah Philips's young mother had died. It was the first time that Troy had to help break the news of a parent's death to a pupil. Sarah's father had phoned Grace with the news and asked Grace to tell his daughter. He would be down to Belling Hills to fetch Sarah the next day.

Troy sat quietly, leaving it to Grace to tell Sarah why she had been called over. Grace spoke so simply, but with a kind of honesty that treated Sarah as an adult and told her all the facts.

'You know that your mother had an operation for cancer a few weeks ago,' she said, taking the girl to sit on the sofa beside her. 'Well, she was not very strong afterwards and it seems that the cancer cells spread before they could do anything more to stop them. Your father was with her when she died, and he said to tell you that she died very peacefully and he is glad that she is no longer in pain.'

'Does that mean my mummy's dead?' the girl asked, her face shocked and white, glimpsing the grief she was about to suffer.

'Yes, Sarah. I'm so sorry. We're all so sorry.'

'Won't I see her again?'

'No, Sarah. It's very hard to understand, but that is the cycle of life. It's the one aspect of living that none of us can escape. When someone as young as your mother dies, it doesn't seem right or fair, but we have to carry on living. This is what your mother will want you to do, Sarah, for her sake.'

Troy felt her eyes fill with unshed tears. She had to clench her hands to stop her emotions surfacing. Sarah was trembling. She looked at both women then turned and ran to Troy, burying her face in her arms.

Troy let Sarah cry until she was exhausted. She had no experience of young grief. She had consoled grieving relatives in hospital, but they had all been adults. She did not really know what to do. Someone would have to tell the girls, Sarah's friends. How would the school react? Would it help to send her home or would it be more sensible to keep her at school, in her normal environment?

Even tonight was a problem. They could hardly make her go back to her dormitory, where the other girls were no doubt jumping with curiosity by now. Nor could Sarah be expected to spend the night in Grace's unfamiliar guest room or on Troy's sofa.

Grace made some tea and they drank from her fine bone-china cups and admired the fluted silver spoons that had once belonged to her mother. Troy thought how clever Grace was to bring her own mother into the conversation in an ordinary way. They were Georgian spoons, and Sarah said that her grandmother had some porcelain dolls which were antique and that sometimes she was allowed to play with them.

By the time it was necessary for Sarah to go to bed, Troy had decided what to do. Sarah was in a four-bedded dormitory. A bed was empty as one of the girls had gone home to have some orthodontic treatment on a mouth crowded with teeth. It would be cramped sleeping in a bunk bed, but at least Troy would be there if Sarah was distressed. And she would be able to speak to the other girls in the room.

They walked over to Troy's flat to collect her pyjamas and robe and toothbrush. Sarah was very quiet, but took some interest in Troy's possessions, particularly the photograph of her parents in its silver frame.

'They look nice,' said Sarah wistfully.

'This flat is only temporary,' said Troy, seeing the tears coming. 'I usually live in the coastguard's cottage by the sea. I have a tree which taps on the window of my bedroom, a whitebeam. It's very friendly.'

'I've never heard of a tree being friendly.'

'Well, this one is. Sometimes I have to tell it to stop talking so I can get some sleep.'

Sarah smiled for the first time. She was a thin twelve-year-old with straight brown hair pulled back in a ponytail and a wide smile, though her smile trembled a bit now. She took Troy's hand.

'You'll have to tell my friends,' she said. 'I can't talk about. . .it.'

'Don't worry. I'll do whatever is necessary, Sarah. And I'll make sure your friends don't keep asking awkward questions. You can leave everything to me.'

Troy dozed as well as she could in the narrow bunk bed under a duvet patterned with the Mad Hatter's tea-party. Sarah slept fitfully and twice Troy got up to comfort her, giving her a mild sedative in the early hours of the morning.

She was so busy the next morning that her feet scarcely touched the ground, and she barely noticed it was another glorious day with scarcely a breath of wind. Sarah's father came for her and there was a tearful reunion before they drove away. The school was buzzing with rumours of Mrs Philips's death, and Grace made a brief announcement at assembly in an atmosphere of shocked silence.

Fortunately half-term was only a few days off and the girls were already riding on a high of excitement. Several girls had left early, booked on flights to join their parents in exotic places like Singapore and Bermuda.

Troy tried not to feel envious. It was not that she was desperate to go travelling abroad. It was because she had a feeling that life was passing her by and nothing was happening. She wanted to feel outrageously happy again and this was not going to happen at Belling Hills.

Normal classes were held on the Friday morning, but from lunchtime onwards a procession of big, gleaming cars came up the drive with parents coming to collect their excited daughters. When the coach arrived to take the train travellers to London, the hysteria mounted.

The forecourt and the courtyard were a seething mass of girls, like colourful butterflies, hugging and crying, hair tossing, making promises, saying goodbye to their best friends, whom they were not going to see for a whole week. Heat rose off the baking flagstones, adding to the stifling haze.

Troy stood outside the medical centre in her full sister's uniform for once, silver buckle on her belt notched one hole smaller. She had lost weight this summer. It was not surprising. There was no incentive to cook in the flat over the science labs, and nowhere to eat if she did cook.

'You're looking very professional, Sister,' said Jonathan, strolling through the crowd to Troy's side. There was no mistaking the ironic tone in his voice. 'What on earth is going on? I could hear the racket a mile away.'

Troy noticed the way the mothers looked at him — thin, tanned females in expensive *haute couture* suits and spiky Italian shoes. She was not surprised. He was very good-looking in an intriguing way, and the weeks by the sea had deepened his tan and smoothed the haggard look from his face. She supposed Grace would have told him about Sarah's mother.

'Half-term hysteria,' Troy said. 'It happens with predictable regularity. The girls are, of course, longing to go home and see their parents, but the wrench of leaving their friends is almost too much to bear. Hence the tears.'

The big coach was revving up its engine to warn the last girls to get aboard. Some were hanging out of the windows, exchanging last-minute confidences.

'You will write, won't you?'
'I will, I will. I'll write every day.'
'Don't forget me.'
'Most of the girls are met in London by nannies or

guardians or aunts for the rest of their journey,' Troy went on trying to sound normal. 'The young lady in the shocking pink shell-suit is a duke's daughter and is spending her half-term in their Scottish castle.'

There was a silent, watchful aura about him. What was Jonathan thinking? Was he missing his daughter? Or had her uniform reminded him of the hospital where he no longer worked? He was about to say something when Troy spotted Lucy's parents getting out of their silver BMW.

'Excuse me, Jonathan. I want to talk to Mr and Mrs Warren and they've just arrived.'

'How is Lucy?' he asked, keeping stride with her.

'She was my only patient at surgery this morning. A stomach upset. She said she had been sick after breakfast, but no one seems to have been with her.'

'Is she making it all up?'

Troy looked at him sharply. 'No, I don't think she is. I think she is genuinely feeling sick. Now, if you'll excuse me, I want to speak to her parents privately.'

'I want to speak to you, Troy. Don't disappear.'

'Now?' she said. 'Can't you see I'm busy? This isn't the time or place for a personal conversation.'

His eyes flashed. 'Did you expect an apology?'

'Were you going to make one?'

'I hadn't given it a thought.'

'That doesn't surprise me.'

Troy caught up with Mr and Mrs Warren. She spoke to them for a few minutes, explaining that Lucy had been ill that morning but was well enough to go home.

'We've thought about what you suggested,' said Mrs Warren. 'We're going to take Lucy to the factory. She might be interested in helping us with our market research. It means going through all our competitors' catalogues and marking what looks good and what looks tacky. She had good taste.'

'That sounds a terrific idea,' said Troy.

Mrs Warren looked apologetic. 'We are not *haute couture*. We supply mail-order firms. Very middle-of-the-road.'

Troy touched the woman's arm quickly. 'There's nothing wrong with that. You fill an important role in the lives of many families. Don't be ashamed of it.'

'We make a very good living.' Mrs Warren glanced with pride at their car and the stately school building in the background.

'I'll fetch Lucy. She's been lying down in the medical centre. Tell her about helping you. I'm sure she'll be pleased.'

'Thank you, Sister. We do appreciate your help.'

Troy smiled. She felt tired and drained. She had not realised how much she needed this half-term, but what was she going to do with it? All last year she had stayed in the coastguard's cottage and taken long coastal walks, or inwards along the river estuaries and up on to the barren heights.

But there was no incentive to stay in the attic flat. She longed to get out of its claustrophobic clutches. But where could she go? She had no relations, no money to stay at a hotel.

There was a commotion by one of the cars. A young woman lay on the ground. She had fainted in the heat.

'Please carry her into the medical centre,' said Troy quickly to the husband. The woman was breathing normally and was already beginning to regain consciousness. 'It's much cooler inside.'

The woman fluttered her eyes and saw Jonathan peering over her. 'Doctor. . .' she said weakly.

'Don't worry,' he said smoothly. 'You're in good hands.' He turned to Troy, lowering his voice. 'Low blood-sugar, maybe low blood-pressure?'

Troy elbowed Jonathan out of the way. 'Mrs Patterson is pregnant. She has been standing too long in the sun. I can cope, if you don't mind.'

Another parent made a bee-line towards Troy. 'Sister, I wonder if I could have a word about my daughter. . .?'

Troy listened, nodded, reassured. There were always so many small problems to attend to. She tried to remember everything so that she could put notes on her computer.

'Now can I talk to you or do I have to make an appointment?' Jonathan's mouth curved, hinting at sardonic humour and veiled hostility.

The seamless sun beat down with unrelenting heat. Troy's uniform was hot and heavy, and she longed to change.

'Have you finished here?' he went on relentlessly. 'I fancy a long, cold beer in a riverside pub. How about you? It means I have to ask you to drive.'

Troy was tempted by the thought of getting away from the school, the children and the demanding parents to do something nomal like having a drink in a pub.

'Give me twenty minutes. I'll come down for the car.'

'It's here.'

'Where?'

He pointed to where the low-slung car was parked in the distance, close to her flat.

'My hands are improving. I drove it up here this morning before the crowds started to arrive. I thought a little practice on a private road was a good idea.'

Without thinking, she took hold of both his hands and flexed the fingers. She could feel a reaction, a strength coming back. His fingers curled round hers, holding her hand in a firm grip, his touch sending a tremor through her even in that public place.

'They're looking better,' she said.

'Improving, eh? Still not steady enough for a knife.'

Troy winced. 'Can't hurry nature. Have faith.'

She fled upstairs to her flat. She showered quickly, and changed into a thin butterscotch silk dress and sandals. She brushed her hair until it shone like a glossy curtain.

She knew where she would take Jonathan. It was an old coaching-inn high on the hill, overlooking the Dartmouth estuary. They would be able to sit in the garden and watch the river boats paddling up and down. It would be perfect at this time of day.

The terraced garden was choking with tubs of bright geraniums and lobelia growing in cascades. They sat at a wooden table enjoying the view, watching a kestrel hovering near by like a great brown and white butterfly. Across the river, on the other shore, they could see an invasion of rhododendron bushes taking hold below a tiny hamlet.

Jonathan came back from the bar with two long

glasses — a St Clements for Troy, beer for himself. Troy noted the confident way he was holding the glasses, being careful not to draw attention to the improvement.

'What are you going to do for half-term?' he asked.

'I haven't given it a thought,' she said, deliberately keeping her voice cool. 'I hoped you might be moving out of my cottage.'

'Negotiating my car a few yards slowly up the school drive doesn't qualify me for driving back to London.'

'They've built a railway, or hadn't you noticed?'

'Aren't you going to visit your husband?'

The question caught Troy by surprise. They'd successfully ignored the subject since that time in the pool, when she had told Jonathan that she had been married. Something had stopped her telling him the whole truth. She had deliberately let him think Peter was still around. It seemed easier at the time.

'No,' she said carefully. 'He's halfway across the world and I doubt if he would be overjoyed to see me. He traded me in for a new model, a very expensive new model. It all happened very quickly. One minute I was married, and the next I didn't even have a roof over my head.'

'You're not still married?'

'No, I was made redundant. No longer required. I'd reached my sell-by date.'

'Does that mean you're divorced?'

'Irrevocably. He got rid of me as fast as humanly possible. It was hardly decent.'

'No wonder you dislike men. But we aren't all like that. Some of us would like to stay married to the same woman for the whole of our life.' He glanced around the garden as if momentarily embarrassed. 'Look, Troy, I was going to say this anyway. I have a very pleasant house in Holland Park. I could give you a key. Why not go to London for half-term, shop, see a few shows? It seems only fair to offer you my house when I've taken over yours.'

Troy let the words wash over her. It was too late for an olive-branch. He had made it only too clear that those passionate moments had been a mistake and that he wanted to forget them. Her pride was suffering. She took a deep breath to quieten her uneven breathing.

'No, thank you,' she said. 'I have other plans.'

'I insist. I'll drop the key round to you.'

CHAPTER SEVEN

GRACE HOWARD had readily given permission for Sarah Philips to return from half-term one day late. This gave Troy a chance to speak to Sarah's classmates first, a task she was not looking forward to.

It was always the same, the first few days of term or the first day back from half-term. A wave of homesickness hit the younger ones and sick-bay was already full of girls not feeling well. Dr Wright was calling by later in the morning, but he was also used to this.

'Nothing a little TLC won't cure,' he said on the phone. 'But I'll pop in to make sure you haven't an epidemic on your hands.'

Troy stood in front of the class, outwardly composed and serene. The week's break had put some roses back in her cheeks and she looked more rested. She was glad it was back to work and that her mind would be fully occupied with the girls' welfare. Jonathan had gone to see his daughter over half-term; this she had gleaned from Grace.

'I want to talk to you about helping Sarah get used to being without her mother. Naturally Sarah is very upset, but she won't know what to say if twenty of you rush over to say how sorry you are. If you all crowd round, it'll make it very difficult for her to keep calm. I suggest that your class monitor says, in a few simple words, how sorry everyone is, and no more. Try to be normal and natural for the rest of the day. Don't stare at her. Show her that school is just the same as usual.'

Troy looked at the rows of young faces, some already close to tears. It wouldn't take long for the whole class to go to pieces.

'Who is Sarah's best friend?' Troy asked.

'I am, Sister. Elise Velesque.'

'Well, Elise, if Sarah gets upset in class I want you, and only you, to comfort her and if necessary take her outside to the gardens or to the cloakroom. It won't help Sarah if a herd of you stampede around her.'

There were a few suppressed giggles.

'I'll do that,' said Elise. 'I'll help all I can.'

'Good,' said Troy. 'The way to help Sarah is by showing sympathy, sharing her grief, but also by being as normal as possible. Be funny if you want to. It doesn't hurt to laugh. A joke doesn't mean that you don't care. I know a lot of you have sent her beautiful cards, and I'm sure she appreciates them. Show Sarah that the class is just the same as before she left to go home. The school is like a second family and we all have strong feelings when a member of that family experiences death. We have a chance now to. . .'

Troy broke off. Her sharp ears had picked up the sound of footsteps coming up the stairs. She put a smile on her face. 'I think I can hear Sarah coming along now. Make her feel welcome, but remember, no big fuss. Elise. . .do you want to go and meet your friend outside first?'

The teacher signalled a discreet 'Well done' to Troy with her eyebrows and switched on the overhead projector for the beginning of class. 'Page twenty-nine, girls. The Ganges delta,' she said.

Troy grimaced and went out of the classroom. She saw the two girls talking closely in the corridor as she hurried downstairs to go back to the sick-bay. The cleaning staff were busy in the medical centre, so Troy had not been too concerned about leaving her small patients for ten minutes.

She met Jonathan on the way, almost bumping into him round a corner. Suddenly he was there, tall and powerful, close to her dazzled face, and she could smell the scent of his wet skin. He had been swimming. For a moment, she could not think, her face drained of colour. She had seen him several times since their pleasant truce-like riverside drink before half-term, and as their eyes met she felt a pang in her heart. She could not trust herself to speak.

'I hear you've got a full house,' he said, filling the gap. 'Grace told me.'

'Homesickness. It always happens.'

'Do you mind if I have a look?'

Troy bridled, stepping sideways as if to pass him. 'There's no need. Dr Wright is on his way.'

'Ah. . .your youthful admirer. Still, it wouldn't hurt to have two opinions. Please be sensible, Troy.'

'We seem to have had this conversation before, Jonathan. This is my medical centre and I will not tolerate any interference. I know you are top of your profession, but none of the girls needs hip replacements.'

'What would your precious parents say if they heard you turned down an offer from a London-based medical consultant two hours before the arrival of your local GP? Admit it, now, Troy—they wouldn't be very pleased. And Roger Wright can't possibly get here until his morning surgery is over.'

'I suppose you're right,' said Troy reluctantly. 'But you'll find them all reading or playing cards. Not exactly life-threatening situations.'

But the sick-bay was in an uproar. Caroline McNeil was being very sick and the cleaning lady was doing her best. The other girls were clearly upset, and Troy quickly drew the curtains round the poor white-faced Caroline.

'Thank you, Evie. You've done everything possible. I'll cope now and I have Dr Howard with me.'

'Thank goodness you're here, Sister. The wee girlie is in dreadful pain.'

Jonathan was so gentle in his examination of the frightened girl. Troy could only approve of the way he explained everything and asked questions. He noted and carefully palpated the tender and swollen abdomen.

'Have you had any pain like this before, Caroline?'

'Y-Yes. . .'

'Last week?'

'Yes. . .several times.'

'Did you tell your parents?'

'I went to bed and took an aspirin.'

'But did you tell your mother?'

Caroline turned away to be violently ill again. Troy washed her and put cool cloths on her forehead. Eventually the girl lay back on the pillows and shook her head. 'No. She was too busy. She runs a business. I didn't like to bother her.'

Jonathan beckoned Troy outside the curtains. 'I think that young lady ought to be in hospital under observation. It looks like inflammation of the appendix. May I use your phone?'

'Of course. Thank you, Jonathan — not exactly acute homesickness.'

'I'll go along in the ambulance with Caroline. You've got your hands full. I might be able to fit in some physio while I'm at the hospital. They are always very accommodating.'

He lounged negligently against the door. He had only to walk into any physiotherapy department to be surrounded by offers of treatment. Troy had seen stars shining in the physio's eyes at having such a charismatic patient.

Troy busied herself, not wanting to look at him, finding his expression hard to read. 'I'll tell Caroline what's happening and pack a few things for her in a bag.'

It was one of those days. A long line of girls waited for the opening of her surgery. Had they been saving everything up for their return to school? There was earache, headaches, cuts and bruises and a very nasty torn nail.

'How on earth did you do that?' asked Troy.

'Trying to get my tuck-box open,' said the girl, near to tears. 'My brother had stuck it down with super-glue.'

'Charming.' Carefully Troy cleaned up the soggy mess, trimmed the torn nail, and put on a dressing and protective leather sheath.

'Try not to use that finger at all; especially don't

knock it and don't get it wet. Come back for a fresh dressing every day and we'll see how it goes.'

'Can't I wash, Sister?' This was no grubby little boy, but a squeaky-clean young girl who looked absolutely dismayed at the thought of not washing.

'Everywhere except that finger,' Troy smiled. 'Put a plastic bag on it. Get your friends to help you. They'll love it. A good excuse to get out of a study period.'

A verruca arrived. It was a flat, hard lump of roughened skin on the sole of a girl's foot, and very infectious. Troy hoped that the infection was not in the school pool, but the girl said her brother also had one and it might be their pool at home.

'Sorry, no swimming for you, until this has cleared up,' said Troy. She applied a keratolytic agent in the form of a cream then put on an adhesive dressing for the girl's comfort.

At some time during the morning Troy managed to grab a cup of coffee and straighten the sick-bay before Dr Wright arrived. He came breezing in, his eyes lighting up as he saw Troy in her trim blue tunic and trousers, her hair twisted back in a pretty clip.

'Hello, Sister. Good half-term? I meant to call you.'

'I was out a lot.'

'Lucky for some. Now where are my patients?'

'Caroline McNeil has already gone to hospital by ambulance with suspected appendicitis. She was in a lot of pain, and her lower right abdomen was tender to the touch.'

Troy explained the situation and how she had not been able to refuse additional medical help.

'Quite right,' said Roger solemnly. 'I'll see what's happening at the hospital on my way back.'

He was able to reassure Troy that her other patients were well on the way to recovery and could return to their classes the following day. Troy should keep them busy with books and games, and give them no food, just liquids. They would soon be hungry and longing to get back to their normal routine.

After the usual cup of coffee and biscuits, Roger went to leave but hesitated, his face flushed. 'The cricket club are having a dance at the Cliff Hotel in a couple of weeks, Troy. Would you like to come? Very casual. Might be fun.'

Troy was caught between a sudden urge to go out, to dance, to be part of a normal social scene, and her reluctance to encourage the young doctor. She knew he liked her. She knew she would enjoy his company, but he would read far more into it. She had no wish to find herself in a situation where she had to hurt him.

'How lovely,' she said warmly. 'But can I let you know? I don't know what's happening yet.'

She made it sound as if she might be working. Roger looked pleased with even half a hope. Oh, dear, Troy thought, why do people fall for the wrong people?

Troy managed to find time to go into the staffroom at lunch time and give the teachers up-to-date news about their pupils. Ada Lawson caught her arm as she was leaving.

'Troy, have you any idea what's the matter with Lucy Warren? I can't make out that girl. She doesn't seem to be able to concentrate on anything in class, and yet I'm sure she's quite bright.'

Troy looked at her uncertainly. 'I wish I did know, Ada. I've spoken to her parents twice and they were unaware that there was any problem. Perhaps she ought to have a full medical examination in case there's something we haven't spotted. Yet I don't want to alarm Lucy unnecessarily. She's a very sensitive girl.'

'It's all so vague,' said Mrs Lawson. 'Sometimes I wonder if I'm imagining it...'

'No, you're not,' said Troy. 'Something's not right and it has been noted. Don't worry, I'll keep an eye on her. But let me know if you notice anything unusual.'

Troy realised she was starving. She had had nothing to eat since a rushed breakfast and she was too late for the staff-dining-room lunch. There was nothing but an egg and some stale cereal in her flat.

She sighed when she realised that she would have to make do with biscuits till suppertime. Sometimes she thought she never wanted to see another biscuit.

She caught sight of Jonathan striding back towards the school carrying a familiar white and blue carrier-bag. He had a look of satisfaction on his face, no doubt pleased that he had diagnosed Caroline's appendicitis correctly, wangled an appointment-free physio treatment at the hospital and had his ego polished by an admiring staff.

Well, she would thank him, but she was not going to let him think he was God's gift to overworked sisters. No doubt Roger Wright would have picked up on it as well.

She put her hands firmly in her pockets to stop them from doing anything silly and walked quickly out to him before she could change her mind. How could he look so attractive, be so charming, and yet annoy her in so many ways? She was caught off guard by his arrival and could not make herself indifferent to his presence. She had almost forgotten what it was like to be loved by a man, to feel a man's weight, to give in to that final, soaring intimacy. It scared her that she had forgotten. It scared her even more that she was thinking about it again.

'I have to thank you, Jonathan, for your assistance this morning. I'm sure you're right about Caroline.'

'I was right,' he said complacently. 'I've just checked with the hospital. She's going into surgery now. The appendix was on the point of rupturing.'

Troy went cold. 'Then those couple of hours made all the difference. Roger Wright might have been too late.'

He saw the horror on her face and tried to repair the situation. 'No, not too late, Troy. Don't start carrying a guilt-load. We aren't talking about a life-threatening situation these days, even though a perforated appendix is very serious. What we have been able to do is save Caroline from an extremely painful experience and get it sorted out a good deal earlier.'

Troy nodded, her green eyes clouded. 'Perhaps you'd better come and check the rest of sick-bay,' she said bitterly.

He fought an absurd desire to comfort her. 'No, thank you. I don't want to spend my afternoon playing ludo.' He looked at his watch. 'Have you had any lunch?'

'I haven't had time.'

'And I do want to talk to you...now.' He looked

determined, as if it was something he would put off no longer.

Troy mumbled some excuse about being far too busy. She knew he wanted to ask her about half-term, question her about her stay in his London house, and she did not want to talk about it. 'Another time. . . I really must get some coffee.'

'Coffee! Is that all you live on? Rule one: nurses shouldn't work on an empty stomach. Patients lose their confidence if you faint in a heap at their bedside.'

'It's all right for some. You're on holiday. . .' Swiftly she changed this. 'You're still convalescing. I'm busy. I have a hectic day at everyone's beck and call. Illness doesn't keep social hours or remember that I need a lunch.'

'All the more reason why you should accept more of my assistance, Troy. I'm so much better now.' He held out his hands. There was scarcely a tremor in the hard brown fingers, but Troy knew that it was the grip of his fingers and the steadiness that counted. 'I shouldn't drop a thermometer.'

'All right,' she said, suddenly giving in, rashly. 'A couple of hours a day would be a help. Tomorrow afternoon I'd scheduled to do routine hearing-tests. You could take those over for me. Do you remember how to do them?'

Jonathan grimaced slightly. 'Ticking watch or something. Got any books for me to read up? Conductive and sensori-neural deafness in particular,' he added. He remembered more than he was admitting.

'There's a small number of girls who've been making slow progress, with a slow response to directions or questions. Teachers often think a pupil is day-dreaming, but in actual fact often the child doesn't hear too well.'

'Is Lucy going to be there?'

'Yes, I have included her on the list, although I'm sure her hearing is perfect. Still, one must try everything.'

'And this is a preliminary test before sending a pupil on to an audiology clinic?'

'That's right.' Troy moved towards the medical centre. She already left her small patients too long, though she knew Evie was capable of keeping order for a while. She took a short cut across the tennis courts, and the ground was like metal beneath her feet. She was hot and dusty and her long hair was slipping out of its clip, sticking to her neck. It would help if Jonathan did some of the routine work for her. What else could she think up for him that was really boring? The kitchen hygiene tests? The cockroach count?

'Can I fix you a quick lunch?'

She turned on him, her insides knotted. 'You're impossible, Jonathan Howard. Don't keep following me around.'

He tipped the contents of the carrier on to her desk — smoked salmon, coleslaw, cashew salad and wholemeal rolls. He had brought plates and knives — her plates and knives — from the cottage. He broke open the rolls and began to assemble the ingredients. He filled the rolls to overflowing, and the delicate smell of the smoked salmon tantalised Troy's taste-buds. With a conjuror's flourish, he handed her a plate.

'A Howard speciality,' he said.

'An M & S speciality,' Troy corrected. 'But thank you all the same. It looks and smells delicious.'

'Are you going to come and sit in the sun?'

'In full view of the staffroom windows?' she scorned. 'As if they haven't got enough to gossip about.' She looked mysterious. 'I know a much better place.'

She lead him through the sick-bay, where five pairs of curious eyes followed them, and went through the open French doors at the other end. It led out on to a small walled garden with tiny flowerbeds full of pink and white candytuft, mauve asters, a magnolia tree for shade and an old stone sundial.

'This is a special place for my convalescing patients,' said Troy with enthusiasm. 'There's fresh air and privacy, and it helps them make the difficult step from being ill back to the classroom. Even in winter they like coming out here and pottering around, feeding the birds or sweeping the little path for me. Being ill at school is so different from being ill at home.'

'It's perfect,' he said, stretching out on the grass under the drooping magnolia. 'You're a very clever lady. You know a lot about children, don't you? And you actually like them. It shows in everything you say and do.'

'I've learned most of it since I came here. Grace, of course, is marvellous with the girls, and I've watched her dealing with them. But being headmistress doesn't give her the same opportunities to really know them. When the girls come to me, they are at their lowest ebb.'

He nodded thoughtfully, taking a bite of his roll, curling a sliver of smoked salmon with his tongue. 'I know a certain young lady who has never been at a low ebb in her entire life. She's spent her twelve years of living on a perpetual high. She's like a one-girl unstoppable roller-coaster.'

Troy laughed. 'And who is this little monster?'

An errant breeze stirred the magnolia tree, and the last few waxen petals floated to the ground. For a moment Troy felt unbearably sad. She loved the elegant beauty of the magnolia, though this was not a tree that talked to her. The pinky-ivory flowers were so exquisitely shaped, unlike any other flowers. And now they had all gone and the tree had lost its finery.

'Troy, I want to talk about her. Her name is Amanda. Amanda actually means "worthy of love", and I have to say she was totally misnamed. She has so much energy, most of it misdirected. She is out of control. No one can handle her.'

'Sounds like an allergy case to me,' said Troy, only half listening, not able to place an Amanda in the school. It was so peaceful in the walled garden. She could hear a bee buzzing among the flowers and a faint rustle among the branches as a bird hunted for insects. It seemed that even the heat had a sound. 'Has she been tested for gluten or eggs or milk? Hyperactivity often stems from an allergic reaction.'

'Is that all you can say?' said Jonathan angrily. 'Just another case to you?'

Troy looked bewildered at his sudden change of mood. 'But I thought this was just another case. I thought we were talking shop.'

'No, we were not talking shop. Amanda happens to be important to me——'

They were interrupted by Troy's bleeper going off. Without a word she scrambled to her feet and hurried indoors to a telephone. She tucked her hair behind her ear and picked up the receiver. 'Hello? Sister Kingsbury speaking. . .'

She listened intently. 'Now don't panic, Lydia. Get Joe to fetch the longest ladders we have. And keep the girls out of the way. We don't want an audience. It's not a matinée.'

Troy hurried into the surgery to pick up her medical bag and a small portable oxygen cylinder. There was no time to lose, and no way of getting out of the most disagreeable part. She was going to have to ask Jonathan to help.

She went back to the walled garden. Jonathan looked as if he was asleep, arms folded behind his head, the sun playing on the angular planes of his face. She moved closer, unable to resist an opportunity to inhale his own special, musky aroma. He snapped open his uncomfortably bright blue eyes.

'Is this some kind of proposition?' he drawled.

'Yes,' she said, but not in the tone he expected. 'Could you climb a ladder up to the second floor and break a window into the girls' cloakroom? One of the girls has locked herself in and she's having an asthma attack. I hate asking you.'

'I bet you do, but I'm glad to see you're on bended knee. That's how I like to see all suppliants.'

'Please stop talking nonsense and come and help. It's urgent. Drusilla is having severe breathing problems. One of us has got to get in. Joe is trying to get the door off its hinges, but it might be quicker just to shin up a ladder and break the window. I've two salbutamol inhalers. You take one of them and I'll take the oxygen.'

'Why is she locked in the cloakroom?' Jonathan asked as they hurried over to the main school, where a small group of staff had gathered under the ladders. 'Can't she open the door?'

'She's been smoking, I think. If she's caught, she could be expelled. She was taking a gamble with her asthma and if we don't hurry she'll be in real trouble.'

She saw Jonathan clenching his hands and realised for the first time what she had asked him to do. He was doubting if his hands would manage to grip the rungs. She had a sudden vision of him slipping, falling to the ground, and her heart almost stopped beating with the pain. She glanced at his strongly carved jaw, the dark lashes, and knew he must not do it.

'Second thoughts,' she said cheerfully. 'I'll go up the ladder. You help Joe with the door.'

'Damn your second thoughts,' he growled. 'I'm not an invalid. I'm going up the ladder.'

CHAPTER EIGHT

TROY could not take her eyes off Jonathan as he climbed the ladder up to the second floor. He was no Superman with superhuman powers, but a vulnerable human being. She was frozen to the ground, her heart pounding like a hammer. The ladder did not look long enough, strong enough, wide enough. Though Jonathan was physically strong, she knew his hands might fail him.

Everything vanished around Troy. It seemed that there were only the two of them, and even the sun conspired to dazzle her eyes so that she could not follow Jonathan's progress.

Grace appeared at her side, composed and unruffled in her usual pale grey suit. She could have been at the annual sports day with Jonathan taking part in an obstacle race.

'Who has locked herself in the second floor cloakroom, Troy?'

'It's Drusilla Huth, Grace, from the fourth year. She's an asthma sufferer, though it's improved since she started swimming regularly.'

'Is she having an attack now?'

'Apparently. Joe said he could hear her wheezing.'

'Then shouldn't you be upstairs in case Joe manages to get the door open first? There's no need for you to watch my brother climbing a ladder. He's been climbing trees since the day he could walk, and fallen out of dozens without coming to any harm.'

'But his hands...'

'Jonathan knows what he's doing. He doesn't take unnecessary risks in any situation. I know he has a reputation for taking chances in Theatre, but he always knows the options.'

'But I don't think I gave him any option,' said Troy drily, annoyed with herself for letting Grace see her concern.

She hurried up to the second floor, where Joe, red in the face, was trying to force off a hinge that had rusted solid with age. She could hear the girl's wheezing, a horrid rasping sound with noisy breathing. Any second now the girl would start to panic

'Can you unlock the door, Drusilla?' Troy shouted, but keeping her voice calm. It was probably too late for the girl to be capable of doing anything. 'Now sit up and keep sitting up. Lean forward against the washbasin if possible. That'll help you to breathe more easily. Have you got your inhaler with you?'

She obviously hadn't. When an asthmatic had prescribed treatments so many times a day, there was no need to carry an inhaler around. Troy felt a failure. She thought she had got the message across in her health and hygiene talks, but here was a girl smoking in secret. How many more were there in the school? Perhaps this episode would give them the short, sharp warning they needed.

'It's coming,' Joe groaned above the splintering of wood. Just as the hinge began to loosen, Troy heard the lock go back, and the door swung open. Jonathan loomed large in the doorway, panting, perspiration dewing his forehead, his shirt sleeve torn.

'Get that oxygen in quick,' he said. 'Then I'll give her five minims of one in one thousand solution of adrenaline.'

The girl was pale and clammy with a distinct blue tinge to her mouth. She had managed to drag herself into a sitting position on the floor. Troy did everything at once, at twice the speed of light. She helped administer a few whiffs of life-saving oxygen, found a hypodermic pack, and broke the seal.

'Steam,' said Troy, turning on the hot tap. 'Always helps.'

Troy heaved the girl into a better position so that her breathing was not so cramped.

'Can you get a chair quickly, please, Joe?' They lifted Drusilla into the most comfortable position, which was sitting the wrong way round on the chair, leaning forward over the back. By now the terrible wheezing was easing and Drusilla was able to use her normal inhaler, with help from Troy.

'She can have one repeat dose,' said Jonathan. 'If she doesn't improve then, I think we ought to get her to hospital.'

The girl was making desperate efforts to control her breathing. She was really worried about the effects of the smoking and how much trouble she was in at school.

'Shall I. . .be expelled?' she gasped.

'Don't worry about that now,' said Troy. It was such a waste. The girl was a bright student with a future.

'Give her a few more minutes and see how she is.

Her colour is coming back. You're doing very well, Drusilla,' said Troy, reassuring her. Her eye was caught by splashes of red on Jonathan's shirt. 'You're bleeding. . .'

'It's just a scratch. Caught my arm on some glass as I climbed through the window.'

'I'll see to it.'

'Not now, Sister. One patient at a time.'

Troy's spirits rose as Drusilla's breathing improved and there was no need to call an ambulance. Twice in one day would have given the school a bad reputation. There was a spare bed in the sick-bay and soon Drusilla was installed among all the ludo-playing first years, who were getting over their homesickness rapidly and counting the minutes to teatime.

Troy could hardly believe that it was still the same day. She felt like a hamster racing round and round its little wheel getting nowhere. Evening surgery was just as busy. She was thankful to have Jonathan's assistance and his advice.

Jonathan's wound was only a scratch. He merely bled in a healthy way. But she did probe carefully for any fragments of glass before she cleaned it up and slapped on a large square of plaster.

'You'll live,' she said, giving his arm a friendly pat.

'No medal for valour?' he asked, rolling down his sleeve. 'Head for heights? Devotion to duty?'

'Grace tells me you were always shinning up trees.'

'I believe in practising my skills.'

Had he been practising his kissing on her? Perhaps that was all those kisses had been. . .a means of keeping his hand in away from the fruitful hunting-ground of the big hospital.

'You were pretty smart, too. I've never seen any nurse work so fast. I wish you were on my theatre team.'

Troy forced a smile. 'I've never done much theatre work. I like my patients conscious and vocal. Establishing that one-to-one relationship is important.'

Suddenly Jonathan took her hand in a gesture that was tender and forceful. She was filled with a wild longing for a more intimate touch. She was aching with desperation to taste his mouth on hers again, floating in that dream-world that he always created for her. His kisses were like a drug. She still had not mentioned half-term and the offer of his house in London.

'I must go,' he said awkwardly. 'I've got to meet someone for tonight's party. She hates waiting. She's liable to bring BR out on strike.'

'Oh, dear, then I wouldn't dream of delaying you. I know how you hate being late for anything,' said Troy. 'The arm is only a scratch. It shouldn't hinder your social life.'

Tonight's party. Troy's spirits fell. She had forgotten all about it. Grace was having a drinks party for governors, staff and local dignitaries at eight o'clock. She would never make it, nor did she feel like a party after a day like today. They could hold it without her. No one would miss one quiet, mixed-up, withdrawn young woman who did not know what she was doing, where she was going, or what on earth to do with her life. Tears came into her eyes. She was starting to feel sorry for herself and she knew that was stupid.

She began to tidy the surgery, locking the drugs cupboard and throwing disposable gloves in the bin. A quick call to Plymouth told her that Caroline was doing nicely after her operation. She was so lost in thought, putting the day's notes on the computer, that she did not hear the first timid knock on her door.

'Sister Kingsbury?' Lucy stood in the doorway, hesitating.

'Lucy, my dear. Come in. Surgery is finished, but did you want to see me?'

'No, it's not me. Two things actually. Elise asked me to tell you something. . .'

'Is it something she couldn't tell me herself?'

Lucy began to look more confident. 'Yes, that's it. She didn't want Sarah to know that she had told you.'

'I understand now. Sarah wouldn't like it if she thought her best friend was talking about her, but Elise thinks that I should know something. . .what?'

'Sarah hasn't eaten anything since she came back. No lunch and no tea, nothing. Not even a snack.'

Troy put the jug kettle on and took out two pretty bone-china cups. She was pleased that Lucy had come to her. The girl was slightly more relaxed, but she still had that watchful, uneasy look. She invited the girl to come and sit down, indicating the comfortable armchair.

'I'm just having a cup of tea. Would you like to join me? You were quite right to tell me about Sarah. I don't think we need to worry yet. It's all going to take a very long time and loss of appetite is part of grieving. But if it goes on, I'll want to know.'

'Yes, Sister.' Lucy smoothed her skirt over her knees, sitting primly on the edge of the armchair.

'I'd like to know if she's still not eating properly by the end of the week, if none of her appetite has returned. She might eat very small portions for weeks, just picking at her food, but her natural energy should soon return, making her feel hungry. The sad thing is that when a parent dies sometimes the child feels guilty and angry, and not eating is a way of punishing herself.'

'Shall I tell Elise?'

'Yes, please. And thank Elise for being so observant. I will have a word with Sarah myself, but I won't mention this conversation, of course. It's entirely confidential.'

Lucy smiled. It was the first time Troy had seen the girl smile. It made such a difference to her rather wan face.

Troy poured out a cup of tea and handed it to Lucy. 'And what was the second thing you wanted to tell me?'

'I went to my parents' factory and helped my mother during half-term. Sort of part-time. She asked me to monitor last year's styles in the catalogues, especially the teenage and children's clothes, and see if there were any obvious trends and what looked old hat already.'

'Oh, Lucy, what fun. That must have been really interesting.'

'Yes.' Lucy looked pleased. 'She said I was quite helpful, and I enjoyed it. She said she wants me to come again on a regular basis in the summer holidays and that there are other things I can do. I should like that. Anyway, my mother gave me this for you. She hopes you'll like it.'

Lucy produced a box which she had put on the floor, and gave it to Troy. It was flat and slim. Troy did not open it, afraid that whatever was inside might be tacky.

'How kind,' said Troy, taking the box. 'I'll write and thank your mother. Exams soon, isn't it? How do you feel about them? What are your interests?'

'I might like to be a nurse, like you, or design clothes. I mean, how does one start to learn nursing?'

Troy was only too happy to tell Lucy the various ways of training for the nursing profession. Lots of girls wanted to be nurses at Lucy's age. They often changed their minds.

When at last Troy suggested Lucy should return to her study period, the girl was far more relaxed and almost happy. Looking after Sarah with Elise obviously appealed to her. Troy finished clearing up, handed the sick-bay over to Karen Norwood, and wearily made tracks for her flat.

She wondered what Mrs Warren had sent her. It was a very kind thought and she appreciated that, but doubted if it was anything she would ever wear. She opened the box in the privacy of the flat and at first sight thought it was a black petticoat. But when she shook the garment out, she found it was a sleek black dress, totally understated, in a beautiful, clinging material with tiny shoe-string straps and very little else.

Troy knew it would fit. She knew she would look devastating in it. She had to wear the dress. Any sane woman would want to.

She would go to Grace's party even if she felt half dead. She was determined to wear that dress.

And she was going to make an entrance. It might be the only grand entrance in her life, but she reckoned every woman was entitled to that moment once in a lifetime.

Troy took longer than usual over her preparations, showering and washing her hair, painting pearly varnish on her nails. She had some black silk undies from her honeymoon days, still wrapped in perfumed tissue, that in her haste to move out of the cottage she had forgotten to put with the rest in the loft. She thought it might upset her to wear them, but it didn't. She pinned her long hair into a glossy knot on the top of her head, letting tendrils fall to her honey-tanned shoulders. She put on high-heeled black pumps and cascading silver earrings, and she was ready.

She searched in her dressing-table for perfume, but the bottle was almost empty. It had evaporated. She smiled at herself in the mirror, seeing a slim and svelte woman in a slip of a black dress that did amazing things for her figure. Perhaps Jonathan would not even recognise her. She could pretend to be someone quite different, an uninvited newcomer to the district.

She threw a wrap over her shoulders and walked across the courtyard towards the main school. She could see the lights on in the big bay windows of Grace's apartment. People were moving about, glasses in hand. For a moment Troy took fright. Then she smoothed down the short skirt and drew on her last shreds of courage. Heavens, she was only going to a party, not to the scaffold.

Her heels echoed as she tripped up the wide mahogany staircase to Grace's flat. It was a gracious old building, once the home of a wealthy Victorian merchant and, before that, the country home of some minor aristocracy. The main rooms were all high-ceilinged with ornate plasterwork and huge windows overlooking the high-banked fields that quilted the rolling green and golden Devon countryside.

The room was crowded, everyone talking. Grace caught sight of Troy and came over to greet her, a delighted smile on her face.

'My dear, you look absolutely ravishing! That dress is almost sinful. Oh, dear, it makes me wish I had gone on a diet during half-term,' said Grace. 'Come and meet everyone.'

Troy took a glass of chilled Australian Semillon from Evie, who was also in a black dress. 'Our off-duty uniform, eh?' the older woman grinned.

Troy nodded. 'We must go to the same dressmaker. Reckon she ran out of material though, making mine.'

She laughed and sipped the wine. It tasted of apple with a touch of the sweetness of the grape. Quite delicious.

She could see Jonathan standing by the window in a formal grey suit, the collar of his shirt very white against his tanned neck. He looked so tall and handsome, and her stomach churned at the thought of talking to him. She drank in the sight of him with a lover's thirst. Then she saw his companion and her heart almost stopped.

A young girl stood at his side, long golden hair hanging to her waist like a curtain of corn, slim as a boy in a tight crushed-strawberry velvet dress, heels so high that she could hardly stand straight. A bimbo. Troy turned abruptly. All desire to talk to Jonathan vanished. If that was the kind of female who appealed to him, then it was high time she got the man out of her system. She glanced round the room to find someone else to talk to.

But Jonathan had spotted her and was shouldering his way across to her side. His blue eyes were glinting so hard that it almost hurt to look at them.

'I thought for a moment you were going to ignore me,' he said, his glance sweeping over her like a burning flame. He took in the minuscule dress, the elegant shoes and earrings, the mass of brown hair piled on her head. He sighed heavily. 'You look marvellous. Don't do this to me, Troy. Where has the starchy sister gone?'

'Not very far, I assure you,' said Troy crisply. 'I'm quite likely to go over and tell your dishy young companion that she's throwing her spine out wearing those ridiculous shoes.'

She could not keep the spite out of her words. It was jarring, and she was annoyed with herself. She had betrayed herself with the first thing she said.

'But she is a lovely young woman, isn't she?' he said in a voice so wistful and persuasive that she knew immediately that Jonathan loved the girl. She had known it all along. She had known instantly from the protective way he had been standing over her. Oh, God, this was worse than she had thought. Troy wished she had never come.

'Come over and meet Amanda,' he said, putting his

hand firmly under her elbow. Her hand shook and she was near to spilling her drink.

'Of course,' she said icily. 'I'd love to meet Amanda.' Life was hard and cruel. How many more blows would she have to endure? Her brain seemed to have stopped working and all she could feel was the hurt and the longing.

He steered her across the room and Troy was aware of the admiring glances in her direction. But they did not matter any more. She was tempted to leave, very soon, to hang up the pretty dress and go to bed.

Jonathan removed a glass of wine from Amanda's hand and replaced it with the orange juice she had been drinking when he'd left her. She shot a look of annoyance at him, her glossy mouth drooping sulkily.

Troy saw that Amanda was even younger than she had first thought, despite the sophisticated dress and make-up. She had startling blue eyes and a pert face, but it was her mane of golden hair that was her chief beauty. And the girl was not just slim, she was skinny-thin. Her shoulder-bones stuck out like sticks.

'Amanda, I want you to meet Sister Kingsbury, who works here. Troy, this is my daughter, Amanda.'

Troy heard his words with a kind of incredulous comprehension. His daughter. Of course. She could see a fleeting resemblance in the blue of her eyes, but it was more in the girl's haughty stance and rebellious look.

'Hello, Amanda,' said Troy, taking the girl's reluctant hand. 'It's nice to meet you. Are you staying at Belling Hills?'

'Not by choice. I don't want to, but Dad says I've

got to. I've been hauled down here and dumped in some poky little cottage that's not big enough to swing a cat.' The girl took a drink of the juice and turned up her nose. 'Urgh. If I can't have wine, Dad, isn't there any Coke?'

'You're staying in Coastguard Cottage with your father?' Troy did not know whether to be amused or angry. It served Jonathan right having to live with this spoilt young girl, but she was also angry that her cottage was being used as some kind of hotel. 'It's really very nice.'

'What a dump.'

'You didn't tell me your daughter was coming,' said Troy in a voice she did not recognise.

'I've been trying to tell you all day. Amanda is staying here for the rest of the term.' He sounded both elated and depressed by the arrangement. 'Her grandmother's not too well and Amanda is getting to be a big responsibility for a frail old lady.'

'Invisible, am I, as well?' said Amanda with a familiar toss of her hair. 'Don't mind me. Keep talking about me as if I'm not here. Anyway, I don't need looking after. I can take care of myself.'

'This is a lovely area for walking and swimming. You should have a good time,' said Troy, determined to be polite.

'A good time? You're joking,' said Amanda with disdain, turning up her nose at a dish of snacks. 'I've got to go to school classes like a pathetic juvenile.'

Jonathan saw the surprise cross Troy's face. 'Despite her grown-up appearance, Amanda is only twelve. Her grandmother can't cope. And this is what has happened. Amanda thinks she's twelve going on eighteen. She'll be driving the Jaguar if she gets half a chance.'

'It appears Amanda has come to Belling Hills just in time,' said Grace as she passed on her way to greet some new arrivals. 'My niece will learn a lot here.' Including, her voice implied, not to drink wine and wear layers of mascara.

'Perhaps you'd like to borrow my bicycle,' said Troy in a tone that implied that as Jonathan had already got the cottage he might as well have the rest. It was not lost on Jonathan.

'What a charming thought, Troy,' he said. 'Always the most generous of souls.'

Troy moved on. She felt unbelievably distraught, but it only showed in her darkened eyes. Her smile still worked and she managed to laugh and talk with Grace's guests. She did not want to talk to Jonathan any more. She had to be away from him to digest the reality that Jonathan had been married and had produced a daughter by the normal means, a precocious daughter who was a handful. She also wanted to find out what had happened to Mrs Howard and where she was now. She could only be a gorgeous blonde if Amanda took after her mother.

'Dr Roger Wright,' said Troy, homing in on a figure she recognised. 'How nice to see you. How are you?'

'You saw me this morning,' he grinned. 'Remember?'

'I'd forgotten; it's been such a long day,' she sighed. 'Forgive me. This morning seems like a week ago. I can hardly remember the name of the girl that went to Plymouth.'

'A definite case of mental fatigue,' said Roger, somewhat taken aback by the shortness of her skirt and the stunning glamour of her appearance. He was so used to seeing her looking trim and neat in her blue uniform. She looked a different person and he was a little intimidated. If she came to the cricket club dance in that dress, he wouldn't see her for the stampede.

'You can say that again, Roger. If this is a sample of the rest of term, then roll on the summer holidays. I shall be exhausted. Save me a bed in Intensive Care.'

'Drips at the ready, I promise. Excuse me, Troy, Grace is waving me over. I must obey.'

Troy took another glass of wine. She needed it. How long had Jonathan been married and what had happened? Was his wife still around? Were there any other children? She had a sudden vision of more children arriving, all blonde and beautiful, and a dear little boy who looked just like a miniature version of Jonathan. Tears started into her eyes and she blinked them away angrily, thinking instead of her little cottage bursting at the seams. And where was Amanda going to sleep anyway?

'On the floor,' said Jonathan, answering her unspoken question as he joined her by the big bay window. 'Actually Grace has lent her a sleeping-bag. She's going to have the sofa, which doesn't please madam. She'd prefer a suite at the Plymouth Holiday Inn.'

'It was quite a shock,' said Troy, turning her face away. All reason seemed to have deserted her. She was aware of nothing but his presence. 'Meeting your daughter. She's so. . .grown-up.'

'But I had told you that I had been married and had a daughter,' he said gently. 'Remember?'

'Yes, you did tell me,' she sighed. 'I suppose I didn't want to remember. I chose to forget.'

'And you are just as mysterious about your marriage. You don't tell me anything, so I don't ask. Yet I want to know, Troy. I want to know why you've put up this invisible barrier that is impossible to break down.'

'I. . . I didn't want to talk about it,' Troy faltered. 'It's something I'd rather forget, and I'm beginning to put it all behind me.'

'Perhaps it's the same for me, except in my case the barrier is larger than life and called Amanda. Any young woman being confronted by Amanda at her worst would run a mile. You must admit, she's enough to scare off any smitten female.'

Troy felt her anger melting as Jonathan smiled down at her with those incredibly blue eyes. He was quite right, and it was true: he had been trying to tell her something all day and she just wouldn't listen.

'She is quite alarming,' Troy agreed. 'But she's only twelve and there's plenty of time for her to grow out of this unruly behaviour. Will. . .will you tell me about your wife or should I mind my own business?'

'No, Troy. I want to tell you.' Jonathan paused, marshalling his thoughts. He had not spoken about Louise for a long time. 'My wife was a beautiful creature, a social butterfly, quite unsuited to be the wife of a dedicated and ambitious medic. I was never at home and, if I was, I was too dead tired to go out or take her to parties. So, not surprisingly, she found other escorts.'

Troy could see the pain he was trying to hide. Her eyes filled with dismay as he forced himself to tell his story, and he was obviously reliving the agony.

'Louise was very young,' he went on, making excuses for her. 'She had nothing else to do. We had a nanny for Amanda. She fell for a handsome Spaniard, her dancing teacher, and ran away to Ibiza with him. I don't blame her really. She was too young and lively to be shut away with an orthopaedic surgeon who lived for his work. We were divorced later and I believe she married him.'

'You keep saying "was". . .'

'She was killed in a moped accident. She was riding without a helmet. I suppose it's too hot in Ibiza to wear one, or she didn't want her hair mussed up. She had lovely hair. . .'

'Like Amanda. . .' said Troy gently.

'Like Amanda's.' Jonathan put down his glass and appeared to give himself a mental shake. 'The problem now is, of course, Amanda. She's been living with her maternal grandmother. I went to see them at half-term and found the situation quite impossible. Amanda has been going wild, playing truant, meeting unsuitable friends in the village — mostly boys — staying out late. . .so that's why I've brought her here to Belling Hills. A bit late to play the heavy father. Go on, say it.'

'I haven't said that. But there's something else, isn't there?'

'I have my suspicions. She doesn't eat properly.'

'Anorexia nervosa?'

'She's like a stick-insect. Look at those bones. I'm really worried.'

'It could be that she's just very slim and small-boned.'

'I hope you're right. Have I told you that you're very good for me, Troy? When you're not biting my head off, you have the knack of saying exactly the right thing.'

Jonathan took her hand and rubbed his thumb along her palm. It tickled and sent shivers down her spine. The room was crowded, but it seemed as if there were only the two of them together. They stood looking at each other, seeing the beginning of a strange sort of happiness.

CHAPTER NINE

THE inner harbour at Dartmouth was thronged with small boats bobbing on the deeply green water and holiday-makers strolling along the flower-decked promenade. Troy was finding Amanda's company hard going. The girl was uninterested in the historic port or the castle or the picturesque Butterwalk that had many seventeenth-century houses, each preserved with care. She barely looked at the black and white 1622 charity house in a little alleyway, the old basement door leading to gloomy depths.

'They're just boring old houses,' said Amanda, tossing her hair. 'Who cares anyway?'

'More boring than boring old lessons?' said Troy.

Troy had brought Jonathan and his daughter into Dartmouth in the hope that visiting the steeply hilled sea port would cheer the girl up. The sick-bay was empty and there had only been one pupil at surgery that morning. It had been Melanie Brown, tooth saved and now firmly crowned in position by the dentist. She had severe athlete's foot with broken red skin between all her toes and intense itching.

'Are you using the foot bath before you go into the pool?' Troy asked, hoping this was not the beginning of an epidemic. The infection could spread fast and all the pupils, except Lucy, loved swimming.

'I keep forgetting,' said Melanie, trying not to scratch. 'I like diving in straight away.'

'It's important that this fungus doesn't spread to the other girls, so I'm afraid you can't swim until the infection has cleared up.'

'But it's sports day next week and I'm in the relay team,' the girl groaned.

Troy sprayed the weeping area with a solution of clotrimazole and gave Melanie a quantity of the same agent as a dusting powder. 'Put this in your shoes and socks. Wear clean socks every day. And try not to scratch. Come back this evening and we'll have another go at them.'

'But what about sports day?' said Melanie tearfully, seeing her world disintegrating around her.

'I could suggest to Miss Howard that the entire event be postponed due to the star having athlete's foot,' said Troy briskly, giving her hands a good scrub. 'Cheer up, Melanie. This stuff works. It might clear up in time.'

Troy phoned Lydia Richmond, who was in charge of PE, and suggested that they make sure all the swimmers went through the disinfectant foot bath; then she phoned the cleaning staff to ask them to treat the floors of the showers and bathrooms in the school and the changing cubicles at the pool with disinfectant.

She had been overjoyed to see Jonathan that day. He seemed to be spending a lot of time with his difficult daughter and her arrival had certainly curtailed his freedom to do what he liked. Troy still met him on walks or in the pool, but she missed him with an intense aching.

Those intimate moments at the party had been extra

special. They had talked for a long time, all her tiredness leaving her. He could not take his eyes off her, stunned by her innocent beauty in the slip of a black dress. Their hostility forgotten, Troy's hopes had soared at this new companionship. She did not even mind now about the cottage. She did not envy him sharing that small space with Amanda, and she smiled at the thought. It would be bedlam with that wilful young girl monopolising the sitting-room and the bathroom.

After the party, Jonathan had walked her back to the entrance of her flat, holding her hand lightly in his. The sky was very clear, stars glittering like diamond dust. They had stared at each other, such longing coming from their souls. He had taken her in his arms and kissed her slowly for what seemed an eternity. Troy had clung to him, moving in his embrace, straining for more closeness, her mouth starved for his kisses. She could not prevent herself giving in to his seeking mouth, moving so that he found her ears, her neck, her throat.

'And I've wasted all this time, all this lovely summer,' he groaned. 'Troy, I've been such a fool. And you were right here, all the time, on my doorstep.'

'On my doorstep, you mean,' she murmured, teasing.

He moved awkwardly away from her, reluctantly letting her go, breaking the spell. 'This is madness. One minute more and I shall be removing that delectable dress and then, heaven help me, Troy, I should not be able to keep my hands off you.'

'Would you like to come in for some coffee?' she

asked. 'And I do mean coffee. It's not a veiled invitation. I've no comfortable sofa and only a narrow single bed.'

'You certainly know how to make me feel bad,' he said. 'Let's walk. Look, there's moonlight especially for us.'

'And stars. . .'

'And this time we aren't dreaming. This is for real, Troy. You and me together.' He tucked her hand into his, and his grasp was reassuring and firm. She loved it.

This is how all parties should end, thought Troy, walking through sweet-scented gardens bathed in moonlight with the man that you love and the promise of more happiness. She leaned her head against his shoulder, whispering his name.

Jonathan shrugged off his jacket and laid it on the newly mown lawn under one of Grace's cherry blossom trees. He guided her gently down on to the slope and stretched out beside her, his elbow bent as he gazed with pleasure into her face.

'I want to make love to you so much,' he said, kissing the end of her nose. 'It's only a total lack of privacy that's stopping me.'

'And ants, prickles, tickly grass,' said Troy.

'Damn the ants.' He turned her head and sought her mouth, wrapping his arms round her, pulling her close. He nudged the slender black straps off her shoulders and tasted the sweetness of her skin, his warm tongue causing sensational quivers to run through Troy's body. She turned and twisted in his arms, longing for more, wanting him to find places which would ease the hunger in her heart.

Troy was shaking. She could see that other guests were leaving the party, standing about in the courtyard, talking, finding their car keys.

'This is worse than Clapham Junction,' she sighed, hating herself for having to say it. 'Perhaps you had better hit the road before we shock the board of governors.'

'You're right. Troy, have you got time to drive us into Dartmouth some time?' he asked almost apologetically. 'I wouldn't ask, but. . .'

'Still apprehensive about your hands? They are improving, you know. You might be able to drive.'

'Yes, there's a lot of improvement.' He flexed his fingers thoughtfully. 'But it's a long drive to Dartmouth. What if I break down somewhere or lose control? Amanda's pretty low on sympathy. Troy, what am I going to do with her? I know how to fix bones and joints, but this twelve-year-old has me beaten. I can't get her to eat, talk, do anything. She only wants to listen to the most appallingly loud music and look at fashion magazines.'

'That's fairly normal for a twelve-year-old.'

'Not my daughter,' he said stonily. His gaze was unblinking. Swift concern made Troy touch his arm, and he caught hold of her hand. 'Help me,' he said. 'Talk to her and see what you can find out. If she's anorexic. . .?'

'I will,' she said warmly. 'I'll be free about midday. Would that be all right? There's still this hiccup about her starting classes because of the exams. None of the teachers fancies taking a class of one. Don't worry, Jonathan. I'm sure it's a kind of protest — Amanda's way of rebelling against authority.'

He bent and kissed her soft cheek. His lips were warm and gentle, his closeness momentary and overpowering. Troy could not stop herself. She stroked his face, the outline of his curved lips. He caught her fingers and touched them with the tip of his tongue. It was a moment of exquisite pleasure.

Jonathan left them in the centre of Dartmouth, saying he was going to the bank, then to arrange for his car to be serviced. Troy soon gave up on historic Dartmouth and took Amanda around the shops, and the girl's face showed a flicker of interest in the dress shops and fashion boutiques.

'But this stuff is so old hat,' she exclaimed, fists stuck in the pockets of her torn jeans, baggy T-shirt flapping. 'I wouldn't be seen dead in it.'

'Just as well we have different tastes,' said Troy. 'Or we should all be wearing the same uniform.' She hid a smile. Every other youngster was wearing jeans and T-shirt. 'Would you like some coffee? The café on the corner looks pleasant.'

Troy ordered two home-made scones, raspberry jam and Devonshire cream, but Amanda did not touch hers. She drank black coffee, played with the spoon and drummed restlessly on the table.

'Not hungry? I bet you had a huge breakfast.'

'I don't eat breakfast, and don't tell me it's not good to miss a meal. Dad keeps lecturing me. I'll eat when I'm hungry and not before. He can't force me.'

'Doesn't worry me if you don't eat it,' said Troy offhandedly. 'I'm starving. I'll eat your scone. They're delicious. Breakfast was a million years ago. What's your favourite food?'

Amanda thought. 'Crisps, nuts and chocolate.'

'Fairly normal,' Troy grinned.

Troy drove home slowly through the high-hedged lanes, hoping she would not meet a coachload of trippers. The visit to Dartmouth had not exactly been a success but at least Jonathan had had a few hours to himself. She had caught a glimpse of his retreating back as he'd explored the steep old cobbled streets on his own again, a solitary figure climbing the stepped pavements. He had seemed strangely preoccupied when he'd returned.

A flock of Scottish black-faced sheep began to scramble across the road from an open gate, milling around and baaing like a choir, going in one direction and then the other, a dark dog sleeking between their legs, trying to sort out some order.

Troy put on the brakes and sat back with a laugh. 'This'll take at least ten minutes to sort out.'

'Stupid animals,' said Amanda, hunched up and cramped on the back seat. 'I can't stand the country. It's so boring. And I'm hot.'

'A quick swim, then, as soon as we get back to school.'

'Never. I have to wear a cap because of my hair.'

'Plait your hair and pin it up,' said Troy. 'Really, Amanda, it's all the fashion, didn't you know?'

Amanda shot her a suspicious look, not sure if she was being got at. 'You're just saying that to spite me.

You're always getting at me — saying things about my clothes, about not eating breakfast. I can tell you hate me. You think I'm just a thick, stupid turnip.'

Troy broke into laughter. 'Oh, Amanda, don't be daft.'

'I suppose I'm in the way. I suppose you'd rather be out alone with my rich father.'

'That's enough, Amanda,' said Jonathan sharply. 'Apologise to Troy. You're being very childish and rude.'

'Are you rich?' said Troy, glancing sideways at his stern profile. 'I hadn't given it a thought.'

Jonathan stared at the hedgerows as if the profusion of wild flowers were the most absorbing sight in the world. He had spent a week having pointless disagreements with Amanda, and the thought of how she could dominate his future was making him sick at heart. Yet she couldn't go back to her grandmother. One of the sheep ambled up to the car and stared back at the occupants with vacant eyes.

'And I'm thirsty,' Amanda complained. 'Where can I get a drink?'

'We'll stop at the next McDonalds,' said Jonathan drily. 'After you've apologised to Troy.'

'I noticed a dairy-farm sign a hundred yards back. I'll reverse and drive down the lane to the farm,' said Troy, putting the car into gear. 'They'll sell us some fresh milk.'

Troy didn't wait for any protests from Amanda about not liking milk. If she was thirsty, she would drink it. If the girl wouldn't touch it, then she'd get water from the tap.

It was no show-place but a real working farm, and the yard was cluttered with old farming equipment, with a broken-down tractor, hens pecking in the dust and cats and dogs dashing about in and out of barns. Troy eased the car over the ruts into a parking place out of the way and switched off the engine, totally unaware that the peace of the place was about to be shattered.

'Come on, Amanda, let's see if we can find anyone,' said Troy, ignoring the lack of an apology.

Troy climbed out of the low car and her attention was immediately caught by a group of people hurrying up a nearby field towards the farm. The two men looked as if they were carrying something, and a woman was hurrying ahead of them.

Troy was alerted by the urgency in the woman's pace, and it was obvious, even at this distance, that her breathing was laboured. Troy forgot all about Amanda and began to walk towards her, stumbling on the rough ground. She could see now that the two men were carrying something on a crudely made stretcher of coats and branches.

She turned round and called to Jonathan. 'I think something's happened! I'm going down to see.'

'Written me off, have you?' he snarled in a voice harsh with anger. 'Well, I'm not quite done for. I can still walk. I'm coming too.'

'Don't be silly, Jonathan. I meant nothing of the kind. I was just telling you. . .oh, never mind. It looks as if there's been an accident.'

They opened a wide gate and waded through the

ripe corn towards the group. A man's arm was swinging from the stretcher, covered in blood.

'My husband, my husband. . .' The woman ran towards them, her face desperate with fear. 'It was the bull. . . Jasper. He's been gored. He's bleeding. I must get an ambulance.'

Troy opened her mouth, then closed it, remembering Jonathan's anger. She couldn't cope with this on her own.

'Do that immediately,' said Jonathan. 'Phone for an ambulance, then put water on to boil. I shall need a lot of boiled water. I'll see what I can do for your husband.'

'The ambulance has to come from Plymouth. It'll take ages and he's bleeding something awful. He'll die.'

'He's going to be all right,' said Troy, more cheerfully than she felt. 'Jonathan Howard is a surgeon and I'm the sister from Belling Hills, the boarding-school. We'll do all we can for your husband before the ambulance comes.'

Jonathan made a quick examination of the farmer on the spot. The man was a mess. The bull had gored his chest and his leg and the flesh was in ribbons. His ruddy face was pale and clammy, gaunt with pain.

'Jasper. . .ain't violent,' said one of the farm labourers as he struggled up the hilly field, his accent broad Devonshire. 'It were. . .the heat, I reckon. And the flies nipping him. It wasn't his. . .fault.'

'What is this man's name?'

'George Wiggins, sir. It's his farm.'

'Mr Wiggins, can you hear me? Mr Wiggins? Can you respond by clenching my hand?'

George Wiggins was barely conscious. He had lost a lot of blood and his mangled flesh was a gruesome sight. Troy heard a gasp behind her. It was Amanda, leaning against the car, her face stricken and white.

'Amanda, go into the farmhouse and help Mrs Wiggins boil lots of water,' said Troy. 'Please keep out of the way and try to be useful. Your father knows what he's doing.'

'It would have been better if they hadn't moved him,' said Jonathan as they followed the two youths carrying the stretcher towards the farmhouse. 'There may be internal injuries. I dread to think of the possible damage.'

'People do what they think is best. They didn't want to leave him to bleed to death in a field.'

'I wonder how they got him away from the bull?' said Jonathan, as calmly as if attending a routine minor operation. 'They were very brave.'

'I shudder to think,' said Troy, relieved that, like all dedicated medical men, even one semi-retired, Jonathan did not show any apprehension. 'Down, boy? Or something similar in stronger terms?'

Mrs Wiggins was a little more composed now that she was in her own domain, the big stone-flagged kitchen of the farmhouse, copper pans hanging on the wall. Saucepans of water were already bubbling on the Aga cooker and she had cleared the long wooden kitchen table and was covering it with a newly laundered sheet.

'Not one of my best,' she apologised. 'I reckon I'll

not want to see it again after it's been used today. Is the table all right? I'm not sure. . . Put George here. Oh, my God.' She caught sight of her husband's body. 'I've phoned for an ambulance. They'll be along as quick as they can. Now, lass —' she turned swiftly to Amanda ' — you get busy and make us all a cup of tea. I reckon those two lads who carried George'll be needing a cuppa.'

'This is all fine,' said Troy cheerfully. 'We'll manage.' But she was wondering how on earth they would cope.

Mrs Wiggins hurriedly produced a battered wooden chest from a walk-in larder. She put it on the dresser and opened the lid, her hands trembling.

'You'll be needing this,' she said. 'On an isolated farm like ours, it's sensible to have a first-aid box. There are always accidents of one sort or another, so I've kept it well stocked. I used to be a nurse, you see, a long time ago, and I've kept my hand in on this farm, I can tell you. There's some useful stuff in there. Use what you need for my husband.'

'That's marvellous,' said Jonathan, quickly glancing at the medical supplies which Mrs Wiggins had built up over the years. He could tell by the packaging that some of it had been around quite a time. He tore open packets of lint pads. Troy pounced on the scissors.

'I'd like to help. . .' said Mrs Wiggins uncertainly.

'Thank you, but no,' said Jonathan. 'This really isn't the place for you. Don't worry, Troy and I will take good care of your husband. You make plenty of hot, sweet tea. We don't want you collapsing with shock.'

'I don't want to leave him.'

'We'll call you as soon as he comes round,' said

Troy, hurrying to get everything they would need from the first-aid chest. It was a blessing. She had been wondering just what they could use from a farm kitchen.

Amanda was holding the door open for the youths who were carrying in the farmer. She was managing not to look at his injuries, but her face was ashen. Troy noted the girl's help and smiled her approval.

The youths laid the farmer on the table. Jonathan held pads on pressure points to stem the spurting blood, instructing the boys to find something to raise the level of the injured leg. Troy wrapped a clean tea-cloth round her waist, sterilised the scissors in a pan of boiling water, and stood at the cracked stone sink scrubbing her arms and hands. She took over the pressure pads while Jonathan went to the sink, rolling up his sleeves. With one hand she began to cut away the bloodstained tatters of the farmer's clothes. Jonathan prepared a pain-killing injection, antibiotic, tetanus.

'Mrs Wiggins,' he said, without looking up from his patient, 'it would be a good idea if you took your tray of tea outside or into another room. You can't help us here. Then perhaps you could find Amanda something to do. . .'

'Is he going to be all right?' she said, casting a despairing glance in the direction of the inert body on the table.

'We'll do everything we can, Mrs Wiggins.'

The kitchen was nothing like a sterile operating-theatre, but there was no time to lose. The farmer was still bleeding profusely. He needed a transfusion.

'Couldn't we use his own blood?' said Troy. 'The blood he's losing from the leg is a good colour, clean and healthy.'

'I don't see why not,' said Jonathan. 'We've nothing else. At least it's the right group.'

Troy quickly improvised a sterile container to collect the blood. She fashioned a portable drip, pulling down the old-fashioned clothes airer from the ceiling to create a gravity feed. Jonathan connected the tube into a vein in the farmer's uninjured arm. The unconscious man moved involuntarily.

'That should do the trick,' he said. 'You'll get a mention in the *BMJ* at this rate.'

Troy and Jonathan worked as a team, using elementary first aid, sorting out the mangled leg and chest cavity and tying off veins, but unable to reattach the scores of tiny nerves, blood-vessels and tendons with micro-stitches. Jonathan stitched back flaps of skin. Troy seemed to anticipate everything that he needed, tearing the instruments, needles and thread out of their sterile packs with quick, decisive movements.

'No bones broken, no serious internal injuries,' said Jonathan. 'Mr Wiggins is a lucky man. Those horns narrowly missed the main aorta artery. His leg is not a pretty sight, but he won't lose it. He'll need some skin grafts.'

Troy eased her aching back and pushed her hair out of her eyes. They seemed to have been standing for hours. She glanced out of the window, surprised to see sunshine and rolling fields still there like a Constable painting. Mrs Wiggins had given Amanda the task of feeding the free-range hens, and the girl was leaping about the yard in balletic poses. Troy allowed herself a fleeting smile. Amanda wasn't quite so bored now.

Mr Wiggins groaned. He was regaining consciousness, his colour slightly improved.

'You're all right, Mr Wiggins. You've had a slight argument with your bull. Do you remember?'

'Bad-tempered. . .beast. I won't lose my leg, will I?' he moaned, obviously in pain.

Jonathan reassured him. 'No, you won't lose it, but it needs a lot of patching up—a few plastic veins and some skin grafting. Your wife would naturally like to speak to you, just for a few moments. Then I'll give you something to put you out for the journey to hospital. Your lane is a bit bumpy.'

'Can't afford. . .resurfaced.'

Mrs Wiggins had obviously been waiting outside. She hurried to her husband's side and took his hand tenderly. 'What did you say to our Jasper to make him that mad at you?' she whispered.

'Don't let 'em. . .put that bull down, Martha. He's. . .too valuable,' he replied with remarkable vigour.

Troy had been watching, yet not watching Jonathan through all the intricate procedures. He was painstakingly careful and his hands never faltered, his application steady. His stitching was precise and neat as she swabbed out the blood and handed him fresh sutures, fascinated by his skill in drawing the tattered flesh together. There had come a moment when Troy stopped worrying about his hands. The man was entirely whole again. The surgeon had returned.

Jonathan stood back, flexing his shoulders. The table

was the wrong height for him too, but he was smiling, tired but with a look of satisfaction. He knew too that his hands had not let him down.

Troy tried to clean up the kitchen. There was blood everywhere. They both had blood spattered on their clothes. Her pretty sun-dress was ruined. Jonathan was washing again in the sink, up to his elbows in suds. He held his hands out in front of him, the suds dripping off his fingers.

'All right now, aren't they?' he said quietly.

'Steady as a rock. Nothing wrong with them at all.'

Although she spoke with sincerity, the words echoed like a doom knell in her head. A shudder went through her.

He suddenly seemed to be infused with a great deal of energy, as if he had not spent the last hour doing intricate repair work. 'A few minor ops at first, I think, just to make sure,' he said, almost talking to himself. 'A week or so assisting some great man, then back to normal. Business as usual. Plough into that waiting-list.'

'You're going back to London?' Troy faltered, stunned by the speed of his reaction.

'Yes, tomorrow, I think. No point in wasting time. I've wasted all this summer as it is. I'll get Grace to take Amanda as a boarding pupil. You can have your cottage again. That'll please you and you'll be able to continue your peaceful and untroubled seaside existence.'

But what about me? Troy wanted to cry out. 'What do you mean? All this summer wasted? I thought. . .' She did not know what she thought. 'I suppose it's what you've always wanted, isn't it? To get back to work?'

'Of course,' he said briskly, his eyes dark and unsmiling. 'What else? My work is the most important aspect of my life. This is what I've studied for, taken endless examinations for, worked all hours of the night and day for years. Work broke my marriage and has made me a stranger to my daughter. It's all I have.'

You could have had me, Troy wanted to say, but he clearly did not want her. She had just been a little light relief during a few boring months by the sea. He had already forgotten her in the excitement of returning to work.

'I'll keep an eye on Amanda,' said Troy, salvaging some pride. 'Perhaps talk to her about eating. . . I'm sure Belling Hills will be the best place for her.'

'Thank you, Troy. I knew I could rely on you.'

Good old reliable Troy, she thought bitterly. Everyone's best friend, no one's lover.

Troy talked to the ambulance men as they made Mr Wiggins comfortable and loaded him into their ambulance. They were able to set up a drip straight away, which immediately did something to repair the fluid imbalance. She realised that this was the last time that she and Jonathan would work together on a patient. He was going out of her life, back to his glittering London lifestyle, his high-flying career, his beautiful home.

He seemed oblivious of her feelings, talking to Mrs Wiggins and reassuring her of the outcome, being relaxed and charming, accepting mugs of tea, even teasing Amanda about the chickens.

'I found an egg,' said Amanda. 'Look, it's still warm. Mrs Wiggins says I can keep it and have it for my tea.'

What, an egg? A whole egg? Troy felt like asking if she wasn't overdoing it. But how could she take out her unhappiness on a girl of twelve, who had enough problems of her own, in particular a father who was wrapped up in his career?

Troy drove back to the school in silence. Jonathan did not seem to notice. It was Amanda who chatted now about the dairy, the baby chickens and a pony, and the blood everywhere. She had got over her shock and was relishing the chance to talk about the gory accident to the girls.

'I think I'll go to the school dining-room for supper this evening,' she announced in an offhand manner. 'Troy said she'd introduce me to some of the older girls.'

Troy had said nothing of the sort, but she let it pass. Any remark by Amanda that was close to normality was welcome.

'That's a good idea,' said Troy. 'Sarah, Elise and Lucy are pleasant girls. You may find you have something in common.'

The splashes of blood had dried on Troy's dress. Goodbye, dress, she thought as she hurried upstairs to her flat. She stood under the shower for a full five minutes, letting the water wash away her tiredness, then changed into her cornflower-blue uniform. There was still a long way to go before the summer holidays and she did not even feel pleased about getting her cottage back.

She had not realised how completely she was under

Jonathan's spell, how much she counted on seeing him, how the few intimate moments together had awoken feelings in her that could not easily be dismissed. She knew she loved him.

She wanted him to stay, but he was going. She could hardly plead with him to change his mind or take a hammer to those clever hands. She flinched at the violence of her thoughts and stared at her wan face, eyes dark with pain, in the mirror. She must be going mad.

After surgery she went for a long walk, tramping miles along the coastal path, letting the breeze tangle her hair and bring colour to her cheeks. She watched the sea below pounding the rocks and crags, stroking the little coves of sand with endless waves. She caught sight of a brown head bobbing in the water, a seal making tracks for a different fishing-ground.

Battalions of cormorants were resting on the rocks, drying their wings. She stood on the cliffs worn sheer by the Atlantic's relentless attack, and the colour went out of her world. Everything was black and white with shades of grey.

'What shall I do without him?' she shouted to the sea. It did not answer. She was left to find an answer for herself.

'You can keep the car,' said Jonathan briefly before he left. 'You're stuck down here without one. It's essential. Take Amanda out sometimes. I can use cabs for the time being.'

'I'll get a chauffeur's cap,' said Troy, smarting at the arrogant way he assumed she would still look after

Amanda. But that was his way. She could hardly expect him to change.

She did not see him go and was only achingly aware of the silence he left behind. He did not say goodbye. It was as if he had forgotten she existed. She threw herself into her work, giving more lectures, taking classes and busy surgeries and counselling. At night she slept the deep sleep of the exhausted.

Fortunately Amanda seemed to settle in at Belling Hills and she got on well with Sarah and Lucy. Troy often saw them huddled together in a group. She was also aware that the three girls were eating. They were appearing at meals and eating something. And that was a good sign.

Sunday was Troy's birthday and she took the three girls walking over Dartmoor. It was a long weekend, for a home visit, but they were not going home like most of the other girls. They climbed the rolling hills to the rocky tor called Maiden's Sorrow, and as they panted and stumbled over the rough ground Troy told them the legend of the stone.

'The folk round here say that if you tell your troubles to the maiden, the stone will absorb them — like being porous, I suppose. People come up here just to do that.'

'What a load of rubbish,' said Amanda, picking up a stone and throwing it at the tor. 'Comic-cuts stuff.'

'It does look like a maiden,' said Sarah, surveying the strange formation from all angles. 'She's got her head in her hands and is leaning forward, like this.'

Lucy did not let on that she had been up to the tor before. Grace had warned the two runaway girls not to talk about their expedition to the moors. She did not want a spate of copy-cat adventures. Troy had had to get special permission from Grace for this outing as all Lucy's privileges had been withdrawn for the rest of term.

'Well, I'm going to talk to the stone,' she said, climbing the last few yards. 'You can laugh if you want to, but don't you dare listen. I'm going to tell the maiden a few home truths about unruly boarders.'

Eventually all three girls were clustered round the stone, laughing and giggling.

'My biggest sorrow is that I haven't met Tom Cruise,' Amanda wailed dramatically. 'Or Mel Gibson or Richard Gere.'

'And I can't do my maths prep. . .ever.'

'And nobody likes me,' said Lucy.

Their mirth calmed down. Troy knew that each girl had secret problems and that perhaps telling a stone might be therapeutic. Even she could feel like a daughter of tor, longing to unburden her sorrows to the stone. There was something about the moorland, the scene of many pagan rituals, a timelessness that breathed a serenity into her soul.

'Lunch,' she said. The glorious views of purple moors, distant cropping ponies, the silent standing stones and the vast acres of blue sky were the perfect backcloth. She slipped off her haversack and let it drop on to the carpet of heather and vivid yellow gorse. 'I've brought a picnic.'

The long walk and fresh air had given the girls a healthy appetite. They fell upon the cheese and salad rolls, crisps, apples and nut-bars as if they hadn't eaten for weeks. It was a happy meal and Troy wondered, briefly, if there was any life after Jonathan.

She went to the cricket club dance with Roger Wright and wore her skimpy black dress. He seemed to disapprove of the dress, which amused her, or perhaps he disapproved of the way the other members of the club swarmed round her, asking for dances. Yes, there was definitely life after Jonathan, but perhaps this was not what she wanted.

The weather held for sports day and bloomed clear, sunny and cloudless. Melanie was back in the relay team. The pupils were in a fever of excitement, expectations pitched high, the corridors vibrating with their young voices. Troy knew she was in for a hectic time with the usual collection of sprains, cuts, bruises and nosebleeds, but hopefully no broken bones. She spent the day rushing from one area of competitive sport to another, administering to the wounded in combat.

The last girl at surgery that evening was Lucy. Troy was surprised as she knew Lucy had not taken part in the events, although she had been roped in as a timekeeper and lineswoman.

'Hello, Lucy,' said Troy, tidying up after her last patient. 'What's the matter? Timekeeper's fatigue?'

Troy immediately regretted her flippancy. She had noticed a new tendency to waspish remarks and was annoyed with herself. Lucy was tearing a handkerchief to shreds.

'Come and sit down,' said Troy, immediately concerned. 'Tell me all about it. . .what's the trouble?'

'It's nearly the end of term and I. . .and I don't want to go home,' the girl faltered, looking at the floor.

'Why not, Lucy? You had a good time at half-term, working at the factory. Is it something to do with your parents?'

The girl shook her head. 'No,' she whispered. 'It's cook. . .and her husband. They. . .they. . .'

'Yes, Lucy. . .?'

'They take pictures of me, photographs. . .always have. . .and I don't like it.'

Suddenly Troy went cold. Now she understood.

CHAPTER TEN

TROY discreetly phoned Mrs Warren and asked her to come to the medical centre before taking Lucy home for the holidays. The woman was shocked by Troy's suspicions and said she would dismiss the couple instantly. They had a family holiday planned on the Greek island of Kos, and she would make sure that the couple had gone before they returned. Meanwhile Lucy could stay for a few days with her grandparents.

'I didn't know. . . I didn't suspect. I've always left Lucy in their care and she's never said anything.'

'Children don't,' said Troy. 'They think it's all happening because they've done something wrong or have been bad in some way. It will take Lucy a long time to get over this if it's been going on for some years. She may need counselling.'

'Should I take Lucy to our doctor?'

'It may not be necessary,' said Troy slowly, not sure whether the Warrens would want to press charges and put Lucy through the trauma of reliving all the events. 'I should let Lucy have a happy holiday; the strain for her has been tremendous. Let her relax and feel comfortable and secure at home, start to trust people. I am only so thankful that she came to trust me. Children are resilient. She may recover simply because the threat is no longer there.'

'My poor little girl. . . How could I tell?'

'I've had several talks with Lucy, quietly, in private, in a little walled garden here, trying to adopt a supportive and listening role. It's important for you and your husband to remember not to let any sign of distress or repugnance become obvious to Lucy. She is still your daughter, still the same Lucy. And I am pretty sure there are no physical injuries.'

'What about telling the police? Those two oughtn't be allowed free to do it again.'

'I'm not sure about the procedure. I'll make some enquiries for you. Of course, they should be warned. Ideally they should be punished. But Lucy's well-being is of paramount importance. She comes first. It may be that a warning or court order from the social services department would frighten the daylights out of them both.'

'I can never thank you enough. . .' Mrs Warren nearly broke down. 'If it hadn't been for you. . .'

'The signs were there all the time,' said Troy reluctantly. 'We just didn't recognise them. It's been a lesson to all of us.'

Troy waved the Warren family off in their BMW, confident that Lucy, at least, would have the best summer holiday for years.

And the long summer break gave Troy a chance to recharge her energies, but did little for the drugging hurt in her heart. She had thought Jonathan might come down for Amanda at the end of term and collect his car at the same time, but he sent a chauffeur, and Troy had the dubious pleasure of seeing both Amanda and the car being driven off by a stranger.

Troy had grown fond of Jonathan's wayward daughter and realised that her problems stemmed from years of unintentional parental neglect. Although the grandmother had given her a home, she had been too old and frail to cope with a boisterous youngster. Not eating had been a cry for help.

'Won't you come and visit us in London?' Amanda pleaded, leaning out of the car. 'I shall be on my own. I may well hit the town out of sheer boredom. Dad'll be at the hospital all the time, juggling plastic bones and joints.'

'Maybe. . .' Troy smiled at Amanda's description of her father's work. She still had the key to the house which Jonathan had given her and which she had never used.

In those last few weeks at Belling Hills, Amanda had forgotten about not eating and wanting to look and act grown-up. She'd taken part in every school activity as if making up for lost time, and had encouraged Sarah and Lucy to join her. With Elise, Sarah's other friend, they had become an inseparable four. 'Oh, it's those four,' the staffroom had started to say when hearing of some exploit.

Troy threw herself into redecorating the cottage as if needing to obliterate every sign of Jonathan's occupancy. But when she found one of his books under the bed — a heavy medical tome peppered with markers — she dissolved into tears, clutching the book in her arms as if by magic it might change into the warmth of his body.

He phoned once, late one evening. It was an uncomfortable, edgy conversation, full of half-finished sentences and unsaid thoughts.

'Oh, Troy, it's you. I didn't know if I'd catch you. I want to thank you for all you've done for Amanda,' he began, concentrating on keeping the tone light and casual.

'I treated her as any other pupil, no more, no less,' said Troy stiffly, the sound of his deep voice unravelling her composure. 'Nothing special.'

'I can see a change in her. She's eating when it suits her. She's certainly a different girl. Well done.'

'That's good,' said Troy, wanting to scream. There was a terrible feeling of distance, as if he were phoning from the other side of the world and there was a time lapse on every sentence.

'She's not on the defensive all the time.' There was a pause which Troy refused to fill. She was seething. He could have fetched his daughter at the end of term, could at least have spoken to her personally. Why had it taken so long for him to even telephone her?

'That should encourage you to lower the drawbridge.'

'You misunderstand me, Troy. Amanda is not under any restraint here. She can go where she likes.'

'That's not what I meant. How are your hands?' she asked politely, stilted. Her coffee was growing cold. She stirred it although it did not need stirring. Her hands needed an occupation.

'Working well. My theatre schedule is back to normal. It's a great relief.'

'How splendid,' said Troy, ready to put the phone down, unable to bear this sterile conversation a moment longer. She was feeling sick at heart. 'Thanks for finding the time to phone,' she said with finality.

The receiver clicked at the other end and she found she was listening to the silence and shaking. They had spoken like strangers. Tears spiked her lashes as she drew a steadying breath. She knew she had not stopped loving Jonathan even though he had treated her badly. But had he really treated her that badly? She had told him time and time again that she was not ready for a new relationship, that her broken marriage had left her not trusting men; and now here she was, annoyed because he believed her.

Her friendly whitebeam flamed into colour as autumn arrived and the strong, salty Atlantic winds killed off the last of the flowers in her garden. The sheep left the rough summer grazing and came down into the sheltered valleys.

The autumn term began with the usual chaotic arrival of girls, cases, tuck-boxes, parents, bicycles, mascots, tennis rackets and hockey sticks. Troy tightened the belt of her formal navy uniform and went out to meet the new girls, easy to spot, hanging back and shy as everyone around them greeted old friends with shrieks of welcome. The noise was deafening.

The new first-year intake kept Troy on her toes all day, seeing each girl and building up the notes for her computer records, reassuring parents, and collating ongoing prescriptions. There was a fresh wave of homesickness with tearful little girls clutching much loved teddy-bears and woolly dogs. Troy saw the most distraught, but the main therapy was to keep them busy and have special events for the new ones, like treasure-hunts and rice-paper chases, so that the girls became familiar with the buildings and had fun exploring the grounds.

Troy was pleased to see Ellen, the girl who had been hit by a cricket ball in the summer term, talking animatedly with the girl who had thrown the ball. She knew they had spent part of the holiday together. Caroline McNeil had recovered from her appendectomy and was energetically showing off a new serve. Gillian Pritchard had left. Her parents were sending her to a London crammer. Troy turned her back on the crowd and went into the medical centre. It was business as usual.

It was the middle of October when the storm came. Troy was in bed, trying to sleep, when she heard the rain beginning to batter her windows like steel castanets. She heard the moisture-laden wind moaning, and it did not sound good. A long shaft of moonlight across her bed disappeared as the clouds gathered in a menacing formation, black and heavy. Lightning suddenly stabbed the sky with forked fingers, followed closely by low rumbles of thunder and then a loud clap overhead that shook the cottage.

Troy shivered and ducked under her duvet. She hated and feared storms. She wondered whether to go to the school and check on any jitters in the sick-bay with Karen. There were two little girls with possible chicken-pox symptoms. But she felt sure that her capable assistant would phone if she needed help.

It was a ferocious storm. She could hear the seas pounding below like an angry animal. It was going to be a very high tide. The shape of the beach would change. . .

The shrill sound of the telephone broke into her thoughts. Almost immediately she saw herself struggling against the wind and rain, cycling up to the school.

'Sister Kingsbury,' she mumbled.

'Troy? I'm sorry to wake you if you've managed to sleep through all this. It's Roger Wright. We've a lot of emergencies on hand all round the county. Can you help or are you needed at the school?'

Troy was instantly awake. 'Of course I'll help. I'll check first with Karen Norwood, but I should imagine she's coping with our spotted patients. The care staff are brilliant with the other girls. Where do you need me?'

'Everywhere. There's an old people's home flooded, trees down, road accidents, several fishing-boats in trouble. I need help all over the place.' She could imagine him running his hands distractedly through his hair. 'But there's an ambulance passing Belling Hills in about ten minutes, answering a call from Loop Cove, where there's a lot of damage — houses, boats, cars. They could pick you up.'

'I'll be waiting at the end of the drive. I'll bring what medical supplies I can from the centre.'

'I knew I could count on you. Thanks, Troy.'

Troy phoned Karen, struggling to pull on jeans and a jersey while holding the phone under her ear. A lot of the girls were awake and scared, but there were no problems.

'We're all right in sick-bay,' said Karen. 'The care staff are up and around the dormitories. I'd come too, but. . .'

'You must stay with the spotted ones. I'm pretty sure they're both developing chicken-pox.'

Troy zipped up a waterproof anorak and tucked her hair firmly under an old trilby hat. Outside the weather was appalling, drenching rain flung at her from all directions, the wind bending her beautiful whitebeam almost to the ground. She tried to cycle to the school, but it became impossible. She got off the vehicle and pushed it to the medical centre.

Once inside she filled two medical bags with everything that might be useful. . .bandages, sterile dressings, pain-killers, suturing thread and needles, local anaesthetic, surgical gloves, forceps, tweezers and a supply of tie-on labels. She remembered from her A and E days how useful it was if a patient arrived at Casualty with some information attached to them.

The ambulance was late. Troy huddled by the hedge, getting wetter by the minute. She resigned herself to a wet night and was relieved when she saw the twin headlights blazing towards her. The ambulance stopped and a man leaped out to open the door for Troy.

'Hop in, Sister. Trees and branches on the roads all over the place. Had to make a detour.'

The picturesque harbour of Loop Cove was in chaos. High seas were pounding the harbour wall and it was breached in several places; cars and boats were strewn across the roadway with nearby souvenir shops flooded. Some of the injured had been carried into the old Ship Inn, and at least they were under cover and Troy could work in the dry.

She waded across the road, waves lapping over the top of her boots. The inside of the inn was warm, but there was no lighting. The power lines were down and the innkeeper and his wife were busy putting candles everywhere. The woman brought over a towel for Troy to dry her face and hands.

'I've put hot water on to boil. You nurses always want lots of hot water, don't you?' she said.

'Thank you,' said Troy with a grateful smile. 'But I hope there aren't any babies to deliver tonight. They do choose the most awkward times.'

Troy set to work with the ambulance men helping, sorting out which of the injured needed the most urgent hospital treatment. A woman had been hit by a skidding car and had a broken leg. Two fishermen had been crushed while trying to pull their boat ashore and had multiple lacerations and broken ribs. An elderly man had slipped while walking his dog and was having severe breathing difficulties. They needed to be seen in hospital.

Troy secured the woman's broken leg to the sound one using bandages, placing a well padded splint between the legs. Blankets appeared from the inn and Troy wrapped the woman as comfortably as possible.

'I'm afraid you can't have a drink,' she told the woman. 'You'll have to have an anaesthetic to get that leg set. But I can moisten your mouth.'

'And all that rain outside. . .' the woman joked.

The ambulance men were administering oxygen to the elderly man while Troy cleaned up the two fishermen and put dressings on their cuts. They were both in a lot of pain.

The door swung open and a wash of rain and sea swept into the bar, soaking everyone near by. Two men were carrying in a heavily bleeding teenager. The boy was ashen-faced. 'Oh, God, my arm. . .' he groaned. 'A window. . .blew in.'

'Don't worry,' said Troy calmly. 'We'll soon stop that bleeding.' It was a nasty rip and blood was pumping out. She cut away his sleeve and raised his arm, picking out the biggest slivers of glass with tweezers. Then she pressed hard on the wound with a cloth pad, trying to avoid any embedded glass, holding the gaping edges together. It was so difficult to see. She could clean out any other bits of glass later when she had stopped the bleeding. She bound the pressure pad firmly with bandages, still avoiding the splinters.

A cup of tea appeared at her elbow and Troy nodded her thanks, pushing her damp hair off her face. She had to stop the bleeding before she could deal with those nasty bits.

'Wonderful, thanks,' she said, sipping the hot brew.

The night wore on with the storm raging outside. Troy was too busy to be afraid of the storm. More injured people were carried in as the ambulance took away the first batch of patients, leaving Troy to cope on her own. She got the innkeeper to help her, a quiet, sensible man who was not panicking and had some wartime experience.

Dawn came and threw light on the extent of the storm. The damage to the once pretty cove was devastating. Most of the harbour wall was breached, boats and cars tossed about like toys. Broken branches and uprooted trees littered the gardens of the holiday cottages. Troy stood in the porch, taking a much needed breath of fresh air. Every bone in her body ached.

She longed for a perfumed bath in which to soak her aching limbs and get rid of the smell of antiseptic, then to sleep and sleep. There would be little time before morning surgery at this rate. She realised that she had not thought about Jonathan for several hours. Perhaps this meant that at last she was getting the man out of her system, out of her heart, and that there was some chance of recovery.

A different ambulance crew gave her a lift back to Belling Hills. The landscape was like a battleground, strewn with toppled trees and debris from the storm, with a cullet-grey canopy of clouds. It was heartbreaking to see the lovely countryside wrecked, as if a giant hand had wrenched up whole handfuls of woods and copses and stately oaks which had stood for centuries and tossed them to the wind.

Yet the storm had been capricious. Some areas were completely untouched by the gale-force wind, branches hanging heavy and dejected with the weight of water but still standing strong and upright.

Troy waved a weary goodbye to the driver and hauled her bike out of the hedge. She hardly had the strength to cycle, but the lure of bed and bath revitalised her leg muscles. The school grounds were devastated. Grace's favourite flowering cherry trees were uprooted. She would be upset.

Troy suddenly thought of her whitebeam. The tree wouldn't have stood a chance, growing right on the edge of the cliff, unprotected from the full force of the storm. Ahead she saw uniformed men moving about, putting up yellow tapes across the lane to the coast-guard's cottage.

'What's going on?' she asked, getting off her bicycle.

'Been a landslide, miss. You can't go along there. It's dangerous.'

'But I live there. In the cottage.'

'Not any more you don't, miss.'

But Troy wasn't listening. She ducked under the yellow tape and ran along the lane. She could see her cottage, sturdy as ever, windows glistening, slate roof dripping. She flung open the side-gate and gasped. A gaping chasm appeared at her feet, a muddy slide of earth and rocks, tangled flowers and shrubs. She stared down the hundreds of feet on to the debris-strewn beach, the grey waves rising in angry troughs.

'My garden,' she breathed unsteadily. 'Where's my garden?'

It had disappeared. So had the whitebeam. The whole cliff frontage of her garden had slid into the sea and the cottage itself stood only a foot from the edge. Her heart began to pound wildly. There was still time. She was not going to have her home taken away from her again. She had to get into the cottage to collect her belongings, to save some of her precious possessions.

She opened the front door and went into the sitting-room, her senses immediately aware that there was a slight tilt to the floor. She did not dare look out of the windows in case her courage failed.

A gust of cold air hit her face and she realised that several of the windows were broken. The door opened behind her, causing a sudden chilling draught. She found herself clasped from behind by two arms in a fierce grip and jerked back off her feet.

'What the hell are you doing in here, you little fool? Don't you know the cottage is going over the cliff any moment?'

The voice was angry, masculine. For a moment, in her confused state, Troy thought it was one of the policemen. But her body knew the truth before her brain. Her body recognised the wall of chest, the hard muscles, the warmth, the scent of his skin, was aware of a familiar harshness in his voice.

'Jonathan. . .?'

His grip lessened slightly as her limpness conveyed the extent of her shock and fatigue, her inability to fight him. She turned to him, unable to hide her love and relief. He looked tired and worried, but there was a brightness in his deep blue eyes that she had not seen before. He was everything she had ever wanted in a man.

'Let's get out of here,' he said roughly.

'What are you doing here, Jonathan?'

'Rescuing you, you idiot woman. You're not safe to be let out alone.'

Suddenly they were clinging to each other, their bodies straining, lips moving, hands seeking to hold. Troy laid her head against his pounding heart and let the emotion wash over her. She knew, without his saying a word, that he loved her, or he would not be there.

'Darling,' he said tenderly. 'I was operating till after midnight, then I heard about the storm on the news. I drove down as fast as I could. I drove all night. Then the local radio said there'd been a landslide on this stretch of cliff and they mentioned the coastguard's cottage. And I know you and. . . I could imagine you. . .being absolutely ridiculous about not leaving your cottage and your tree. . . I thought you would be upstairs, sleeping. . .'

'I wasn't here,' said Troy huskily. 'I was at Loop Cove, helping with all the casualties. I've been up all night too.'

He groaned, a sound that was full of anguish and longing. 'I suddenly realised how much I loved you, that I couldn't live a moment longer without you, without telling you, even if you don't want me, even if you hate every man who walks on this earth and send me packing. Oh, Troy, when I thought I might be too late. . .it was agony. I have aged years.'

'But I'm alive, darling. I'm here and I love you too. It's not too late. . .' Every inch of her body reached out to him and Jonathan kissed her with a searing intensity that told her everything she wanted to know. This man loved her. He loved her passionately. He would look after her, protect her, care for her in a way that she had never known.

All her worries and lingering doubts vanished. There was no problem they could not solve together. Suddenly the cold struck up through the soles of her feet. A huge crack had appeared in the floor.

'Out!' Jonathan said urgently, pulling her back. 'It's going over. . .'

'But my things. . .'

'Damn your things. I'll buy you everything you need.'

'My little black dress. . .'

'Haven't you any sense, woman? I'll buy you a dozen little black dresses. If you stay a second longer you won't need any clothes at all.'

He half lifted her off the floor, but not before Troy snatched the silver-framed photograph of her parents from the shelf over the fireplace. Then she ran with him willingly as an ominous cracking sound filled their ears. They ran out of the front door into the lane just as the back wall of the cottage shuddered on its unsupported foundations and gravity took it away in a cloud of dust and cement and rattling stones.

'Oh, no,' Troy cried in despair, rain mixing with the tears on her face. 'My lovely cottage.'

'Don't look,' said Jonathan, cradling her face against his shoulder. She shuddered as she heard the death throes of her home crashing down the cliff.

'It was my home,' she wept.

'Yes, it was your home, home during a very difficult time in your life. But that time is over now,' he said gently, moving as a tree showered them with raindrops. 'But soon you'll have a new home with me. And we'll find another cottage by the sea if that's what you want. But there's my house in London, which you know is spacious and comfortable, just waiting for a few feminine touches.'

'I don't know; I never went in,' she confessed. 'I stood outside on the pavement wondering what to do, but I couldn't make myself go in, just in case. . .in case. . .'

'In case what?'

'I was afraid I might find evidence of another

woman's occupation. . .you know, a scarf, shoes, perfume. I didn't want to know if you lived with anyone.'

He laughed quietly and began to walk her towards his car. 'Little goose. I've never had time for women, never had the inclination, nor even met one that I really liked enough until I met you. You hit me with something more than words the first time we met. You were so angry. A firebrand. I could only watch you and marvel at the way you acted, like a tigress, back to the wall, spitting fire.'

He opened the car door. 'I wanted you to marry me, but how could I have asked you? A man whose career was in ruins, who might never work again, who was on the slag-heap, riddled with guilt over a patient who'd died. I couldn't be dependent on you. I had nothing to offer you. . .'

'A patient that died?'

'In the helicopter crash. My patient didn't survive. He had been very badly injured in a motorway crash, but he had a slight chance. A chance which I denied him.'

'That's not true,' Troy said. 'You said that to me, about not carrying guilt around. And besides, your hands have recovered. You have everything to offer again.'

'But by then Amanda had arrived on the scene. I hadn't realised what a little monster she had become. No woman in her right mind was going to want to take on a stepdaughter like her. Remember how rude she was to you in the car? I decided then that the odds were stacked against me, and I bowed out. I didn't stand a chance.'

'But Jonathan, it was cruel to just leave me. Why didn't you tell me? Why didn't you say something?' Troy asked, remembering all the hurt, all the pain.

'I don't know. I suppose I was plain running scared — scared of being rejected as my wife had rejected me. I couldn't stand that twice, especially when I knew that I loved you so much. And Amanda had become another barrier. How could I ask any woman to take her on? It was all too much.'

'But Amanda is a very normal, rebellious teenager. Belling Hills is full of hair-tossing young ladies with problems. I actually like the little minx, and we get on quite well in a funny way. And I think that a regular dose of parental love and attention will work wonders.'

'Parental? More than one parent?'

'Some stepmothers can be fun.'

She looked at him with a fierce hunger, her skin burning with excitement. He took her hands and moulded them with his fingers, his movements strong and mobile again, promising her infinite pleasures to come.

'Will you marry me, then?'

'Yes. I want that more than anything and I want to make you happy.'

He drove Troy back to the main school and stopped outside the medical centre. He turned to her, wanting to love her, wondering if he dared. He felt strong, confident, full of the inner strength that Troy needed so desperately now that she had lost her cottage forever.

'Do you want to check on your poxy babes in sick-bay? I'll speak to Grace and tell her that you need a day off to sleep. She'll have to find someone else to cope. You can't do any more work.'

Karen Norwood was amazed at Troy's appearance. She looked radiantly happy, her eyes bright with joy, yet her clothes were wet and creased and her hair a hopeless tangle. And she could hardly keep awake.

'It is chicken-pox. They're all nicely spotted this morning. Everyone in the school is fine. No casualties. The storm woke all the girls, of course, and they were having hot chocolate and biscuits at two in the morning. Morning classes are suspended so that they can help with the clearing up in the grounds,' she said.

'Wonderful. They won't need me, then. Perhaps one of the care staff wouldn't mind an easy day in here.'

'I'm sure that can be arranged. You don't look as if you'll last another five minutes.'

Jonathan was waiting outside for her. He was silent, smiling but not moving, his eyes as fathomless as the ocean, allowing her to dictate how this new and wonderful relationship should proceed. He did not want to push her; their love was all too new and fragile.

'They don't need me,' she told him.

'So I guessed.'

She knew, even though she was dead tired, that her body was responding to his nearness. She could feel her pulse racing and her nerves tingling. Troy dared not let her eyes wander over Jonathan's taut body—the broad shoulders, the narrow hips, those long legs that would soon wrap themselves around her. She longed to let her hands trace those strong curves and muscles. . .

'You remember that old riverside inn on the

Dartmouth estuary? The one where we sat in the garden and watched the little river boats go by?' Troy hesitated, but Jonathan did not.

'I'll never forget it. It's a lovely place. Would you like to go there again, Troy? Now, perhaps. . .?'

She nodded happily, taking his hand.

'Perhaps they have a room with a big four-poster bed with smooth sheets and fluffy pillows and a bathroom with a big bath and lots of hot water,' Troy suggested, stifling another yawn with a smile, her desire an exquisite tremor, wanting only to be with him. She must know what it was like to be loved by him. But she had no more fear, no reservations. . . Something told her it would be perfect.

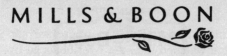

NEW LOOK MEDICAL ROMANCES

To make our medical series even more special we've created a whole new design which perfectly blends heart-warming romance with practical medicine.

And to capture the essence of the series we've given it a new name, chosen by you, our readers, in a recent survey.

Four romances with a medical theme from vets to general practitioners. Watch out for ...

LOVE ON CALL

From October 1993   Price £1.80

Available from W.H. Smith, John Menzies, Martins, Forbuoys, most supermarkets and other paperback stockists.
Also available from Mills & Boon Reader Service, Freepost, PO Box 236, Thornton Road, Croydon, Surrey CR9 9EL. (UK Postage & Packing free)

Proudly present to you...

Betty has been writing for Mills & Boon Romances for over 20 years. She began once she had retired from her job as a Ward Sister. She is married to a Dutchman and spent many years in Holland. Both her experiences as a nurse and her knowledge and love of Holland feature in many of her novels.

Her latest romance *'AT ODDS WITH LOVE'* is available from August 1993, price £1.80.

*Available from W.H. Smith, John Menzies, Martins, Forbuoys, most supermarkets and other paperback stockists.
Also available from Mills & Boon Reader Service, PO Box 236, Thornton Road, Croydon, Surrey CR9 9EL.
(UK Postage & Packing free)*

—MEDICAL ROMANCE—

The books for enjoyment this month are:

JUST WHAT THE DOCTOR ORDERED Caroline Anderson
LABOUR OF LOVE Janet Ferguson
THE FAITHFUL TYPE Elizabeth Harrison
A CERTAIN HUNGER Stella Whitelaw

♥   ♥   ♥   ♥   ♥

Treats in store!

Watch next month for the following absorbing stories:

THE STORM AND THE PASSION Jenny Ashe
SOMEBODY TO LOVE Laura MacDonald
TO DREAM NO MORE Patricia Robertson
VET IN POWER Carol Wood

Available from W.H. Smith, John Menzies, Martins, Forbuoys, most supermarkets and other paperback stockists.

Also available from Mills & Boon Reader Service, Freepost, P.O. Box 236, Thornton Road, Croydon, Surrey CR9 9EL.

Readers in South Africa - write to:
Book Services International Ltd, P.O. Box 41654, Craighall, Transvaal 2024.